MIRACLES IN MY LIFE

LANA O'NEALOVA

This book is about life and the miracles in it. I confirm that all the events mentioned here really happened in my life and describe the miracles that happened to me with the help of my two angels - Lily and Nicky.

This book is written for wizards of the present and the future, for those who already believe in miracles and notice them in their lives, and for those who are just learning magic.

© Lana O'Nealova - 2023

No copyright infringement is intended for reproduction of lyrics used within this book.

TABLE OF CONTENTS

TABLE OF CONTENTS 3

PART I – BEAUTY 6

    CHAPTER 1: GOD EXISTS! 6

    CHAPTER 2: PRINCESS DIANA 8

    CHAPTER 3: DOORS AND DRAWERS 11

    CHAPTER 4: PATH TO A NEW LIFE 14

    CHAPTER 5: THE NEW QUEEN 16

    CHAPTER 6: POETRY LOVER 18

    CHAPTER 7: ENGLAND 20

    CHAPTER 8: A PROPHETIC DREAM 22

    CHAPTER 9: RED DRESS 26

PART II – SUCCESS 28

    CHAPTER 10: LECTURER 28

    CHAPTER 11: PALACE 33

    CHAPTER 12: THE KISS 35

    CHAPTER 13: WE DID NOT PAY FOR THAT! . 42

    CHAPTER 14: SHE IS THE ONE! 45

    CHAPTER 15: "SUNRISE, SUNSET..." 49

CHAPTER 16: DIAMONDS 55

CHAPTER 17: LOSING LEONARD 59

CHAPTER 18: MARISA 62

CHAPTER 19: PYTHON ATE FIVE RABBITS . . 66

CHAPTER 20: DATING SITE 68

CHAPTER 21: 'HI!' 70

PART III – LOVE 73

CHAPTER 22: IT IS HIM, OR THE IMPOSSIBLE BECOMES POSSIBLE 73

CHAPTER 23: THE BLUE MOSQUE, OR FIRST MEETING 78

CHAPTER 24: ISLAND OF HAPPINESS 83

CHAPTER 25: BOY 86

CHAPTER 26: SNOWSTORM, OR MEETING THE PARENTS 93

CHAPTER 27: NELSON MANDELA 102

CHAPTER 28: NOT YOUR COUNTRY 110

PART IV – HAPPINESS 119

CHAPTER 29: HIS WORLD 119

CHAPTER 30: BUBLIK AND BULOCHKA 129

CHAPTER 31: EMILY, OR FRIENDS COME SUDDENLY 133

CHAPTER 32: JUST COINCIDENCES 141

CHAPTER 33: TOWER BRIDGE 144

CHAPTER 34: CAT 148

CHAPTER 35: VITAMIN B12 152

CHAPTER 36: COFFEE AND BISCUIT 161

CHAPTER 37: THE LIFE-CHANGING MAGIC OF TIDYING UP 165

CHAPTER 38: A HOME AND A BUSINESS ... 172

CHAPTER 39: WILLIAM BLAKE 181

CHAPTER 40: BRISTOL, OR THE NEW WIZARD 187

CHAPTER 41: LILY AND NICKY 195

ACKNOWLEDGEMENTS **198**

Part I - Beauty

Chapter 1: God Exists!

When Lana was five years old, her mother taught her to dream. From her mother's perspective, it was a rather cunning attempt to put her daughter to sleep as soon as possible, but surprisingly, it worked perfectly. From that moment, Lana was keenly waiting for when she would finally go to bed and, again, find herself in her own magical kingdom.

This imagined world changed and developed as she grew older, but one thing remained constant: - Lana always dreamt of being beautiful.

She was sure she had the most ordinary appearance. Although boys fell in love with her all the time and dad called her a beauty queen, Lana only believed her mother's low opinion of her daughter's appearance. When twelve-year-old Lana was spinning in front of the mirror, feeling satisfied with her reflection, her mother said, 'A very ordinary girl. Nothing special.'

A little later, Lana started to believe her mother was wrong. She was not ordinary; simply ugly. Once, she refused to go to the cinema with her family at the last moment, deciding that it was better for such a freak to stay at home and not frighten people.

Only in the first year of her university studies did Lana come to realise she was, actually, a very pretty girl, because she was simply bombarded with compliments and male attention. *Dreams come true!* she concluded with joy.

Another event that left an indelible mark on Lana's memory took place the same year, in the medieval basilica of the Hungarian town of Esztergom – where Lana heard the evocative sound of a pipe organ for the first time in her life. Lana, raised atheist in the USSR, was struck by the beautiful music, feeling a tremor rise in her body — and she realised that God did exist!

* * *

At that precise moment, a flock of angels were flying under the dome of the basilica, waiting their turn.

'Another dreamer is ready — Next!' commanded the chief angel.

A pair of child-like angels separated from the flock and flew down to Lana.

'What a pretty one!' said the angel-girl.

'It does not matter what she looks like,' the angel-boy grumbled. 'All that matters is she believes in miracles.'

Thus, Lily and Nicky became Lana's two guardian angels, responsible for all the miracles in her life.

Chapter 2: Princess Diana

It was the last morning of summer and Lana was dancing barefoot on the wet floor. She was wearing a beautiful bodycon dress and the rising sun lit up her long, red hair. The tired DJ played only for her; she was the last on the dance floor. The waiters slowly cleared the tables while her husband sat and admired his beautiful wife dancing.

They had been together four years. He was the business partner of her best friend, who had introduced them. He had clung to Lana from that very first meeting, meeting her every day after her university lectures and ready to fulfil her wishes. She had rejected his advances for a long time but, eventually, his persistence defeated her reluctance. Later, they would become cofounders of the first Chinese restaurant in their hometown of Odessa and running a similar summer business at the seaside on Arcadia Beach.

Lana enjoyed that last morning of summer, dancing in her restaurant on the famous Odessa beach, admiring the sea and the not yet too hot morning sun. Streams of water flowed through the tent, which had leaked over the summer, but Lana did not notice. Dancing barefoot on the wet floor, she felt happy. Well, almost happy – she was now twenty-six but still had no children, and she longed for them.

***

Lily and Nicky were looking at her from above at that moment, sitting on a cloud and swinging their legs.

'Maybe it's time. What do you think, Nicky?' Lily asked cautiously.

'Probably, yes,' Nicky replied. *'I am tired of listening to her moaning at the passing of each birthday: "I'm already twenty-three, twenty-four, twenty-five, twenty-six, and I still have no children!"'*

***

That evening Lana and her husband were invited to a party hosted by one of their friends to bid farewell to the season. It was crowded and fun. Lana danced in her own little world, oblivious to others, while her husband was barbecuing and was the life and soul of the party.

In their relationship, he loved her, and she had allowed him to love her. But, in this moment, Lana looked at her husband and felt a huge wave of love. *I love him! How did I only just realise this? I love him so much!*

Overwhelmed by passionate desires, the two had an unreal night of fulfilled love, crazy and wild as never before, and never after.

The next morning, Lana woke with the firm belief that she would finally become a mother.

While the TV reported on the death of Princess Diana, Lana was completely disinterested. The only important news for her was that she was going to have a baby! She was absolutely certain of it.

Chapter 3: Doors and Drawers

Lana's pregnancy was surprisingly easy. In the fifth month, she learned she would have a girl and immediately began to try and imagine her new daughter's face. She dreamt that her daughter would be an exact copy of her.

In mid-May, around ten days before her due date, it was suggested that Lana go to the hospital, to which she replied, 'I will only go when contractions start, which will happen on May 30 or 31.'

'How can you possibly know?' the doctor asked.

'I just know!' Lana was confident.

'Nobody ever knows, but she does...' But the doctor did not insist, as there was something unusual about this young woman.

***

On May 28, a close friend phoned Lana and advised her to open all doors and drawers in the house before going to the hospital. 'To make the delivery easier,' she explained.

Lana took a lot of calls that day from friends and acquaintances, wanting to find out if everything was ready, and offering to take her to the hospital when the time came.

The contractions started the following evening, while her husband was still at work. Lana and her mother were home alone; no one who had called was available to drive her. Thankfully, her husband arrived a couple of hours later and took her to hospital.

Lana's mother immediately opened every drawer and door in the house...

***

Lying in the ward, Lana was waiting for the terrible pain she had heard so much about. It never arrived, but a baby girl came into the world at two o'clock in the morning.

The first thing Lana said when she saw an exact copy... of her husband: 'You are so ugly!'

Everyone around her laughed. 'You have not seen ugly ones!'

The midwife looked thoughtfully at Lana and said, 'You are lucky. God blessed you with a very easy childbirth.'

***

'Pretty – not beautiful, but pretty. You were born beautiful,' said Lana's mother on seeing the child. This shocked Lana – she never believed her mother saw her as pretty or beautiful.

In the car, on the way home, the girl-child was held by her new grandmother, as Lana was afraid to take the baby in her arms.

'What are we going to do with her?' Lana asked, turning to her mother.

'We will raise her!' her answered confidently.

***

Over time, grandmother's definition of 'pretty' would change to 'nice-looking', and then the new grandmother would start to call the child 'my beauty'. Grandma would become the main person in the girl's life.

Lana would stop worrying about her age, instead starting to count the years of her long-awaited daughter, who came to be known as Freeda.

Chapter 4: Path to a New Life

That summer was incredibly hot. Lana got up early and went for a walk with the baby before the heat arose. She had her usual route but, that morning, she wanted something different and went for a walk in the neighbouring area, where she could hide from the sun in the shade of trees.

On the way back, Lana saw a road she had never noticed before and decided to follow it. The road led to a new high-rise building—white and very beautiful, with green lawns and flower beds laid out in front.

Lana was simply amazed at the contrast between this building and the one where she currently lived. It seemed like another world, the existence of which she had never even imagined. *What a great life some people have,* she mused. The next thought that flashed through her head, though, was: *With my husband, I will never have an apartment in such a beautiful building!*

After the birth of their daughter, the couple had begun drifting apart. Freeda captured all the time, attention, and love of her mother. Dad was busy with the restaurants — he came home in the early hours and woke late. They were like ships passing in the night.

The business they had started together was no longer profitable, but the husband seemed oblivious to this and kept investing time and money in it. To Lana, it was obvious that continuing with the business was a road to nowhere, which caused frequent arguments. Most importantly, Lana stopped believing in her husband, and in his ability to turn the business around.

***

'Did you hear what she said?' Lily asked. *'"With my husband, I will never have an apartment in such a beautiful building!"'*
'Yes, I did,' Nicky replied sadly. *'She no longer believes in him, which means he has no chance of becoming successful while he is with her.'*
'We have to do something!' Lily exclaimed. *'You take care of him, and I will organise an apartment for her. If this is her dream…'*

***

Within two years, Lana became the proud owner of a beautiful, bright, and spacious apartment in the very building she had seen on that walk.
The husband, by then, was no longer in her life.

Chapter 5: The New Queen

After five years of happy marriage, during which Lana had felt like a star, a goddess and a queen, Lana had achieved two university degrees, ran a joint business with her husband, and had a six-month-old daughter who looked like an exact copy of her dad.

Then a new queen appeared in her husband's life.

The news of the new queen was shared by their accountant – an elderly woman, and the only one who had the kindness and strength of character to deliver this unwelcome news to Lana. It seemed almost everyone else was aware but kept silent to avoid destroying the marriage. But, what you do not know does hurt you.

Lana was not ready for this twist. She later realised that she had noticed changes in her husband's behaviour but caring for her little daughter had left no time to stop and realise her crown had been stolen.

Later, at home, Lana sat by Freeda's crib, completely stunned by the news. Despair overwhelmed her.

* * *

Lily and Nicky suddenly appeared. Lily threw open the windows, letting a stream of fresh autumn air into the apartment. Nicky turned on the music at full volume.

***

As Lana listened to the music, she started dancing and singing, and the whole apartment received its best-ever spring clean.

She ran to the crib and shouted to her daughter, 'I will be happy! I'll be happy, anyway!'

The girl looked at her quizzically, with her husband's big brown eyes, and Lana felt absolutely happy!

From that moment on, the feeling of happiness rarely left her, and she started to realise that not everything from the past had to be cleaned from her life.

Chapter 6: Poetry Lover

The night after receiving news of the new queen, Lana could not sleep. Her mind was restless and racing with contradictory thoughts. *How can I tell him that I know everything? Should I tell him? Maybe it is not true?*

As midnight passed, her daughter snoozed peacefully in the crib, but Lana did not sleep. She was gripped by fear, waiting for her husband to return from work.

Emotionally and mentally exhausted, Lana found the strength to get up. She turned on a small lamp and began writing:

> You can't put love and lies together.
> They simply cannot coexist.
> Love is from God, lies are from Devil.
> Why can't you understand all this?
>
> Lies start off like a weed without thirst.
> They quickly bloom and flourish.
> You, too, when lying first
> Think of the feelings that may vanish.

When she finished, she went to bed and instantly fell into a deep and serene sleep.

***

Her husband returned home as the sun was rising. Lana silently handed him the sheet of paper with her verse composed during her long night.

While he was reading, she watched the expression on his face and, at heart, hoped he would say it was all lies, that she should not worry, that he still loved her and only her. But he did not say anything, and no further explanation was needed. Everything was very clear.

***

Nicky quickly brushed a tear from his cheek, but Lily noticed.

'Don't cry, Nicky. You know she is strong; she will survive!'

'I feel like I'm a romantic at heart,' Nicky replied, sniffling. 'I really love poetry!'

Chapter 7: England

The parting was quick. The husband packed up his personal effects and disappeared from Lana's life as if he had never existed in it. The only reminder of him was their daughter. His face, his eyes, his gestures...

Lana was petrified before the divorce. She was madly in love with her little girl, her Freeda, but her husband said he would seek custody as he could provide the child a better future. Staying with him, the little girl would be educated in England.

Lana replied quickly and completely from emotion: 'Yes, the child will be educated in England – but not with you, with me!'

Lily immediately noted this down in her magic notebook.

From that moment on, Lana began to see the same picture from the future, over and over: she is in the apartment of her former mother-in-law, and next to her is a daughter and an English-speaking man.

Was it just a dream?

Lana often asked herself this question and couldn't find the answer. But the fact remained that over the years she continued seeing the very same picture and man.

***

Of course, Freeda remained with her mother and became the main focus of her life, a source of incredible happiness every minute of every day (apart from a few).

Freeda would graduate with a first-class degree from one of the best universities in England… but that story comes much later.

Chapter 8: A Prophetic Dream

After parting with her first husband, Lana remarried quickly, but the memory of the dream she had on the eve of meeting her second husband lasted longer than the marriage.

In that dream, she was walking down a familiar street in the centre of Odessa, but as it was in the Second World War. There was shooting all around and she was very scared. Suddenly she saw a soldier run out from a corner and start shooting at her – but nothing hit her. She fell to the ground, though, pretending to be dead. Numb with fear, she heard the soldier come up to her still body and stand for a while before he left.

Lana woke bathed in a cold sweat. The dream was so realistic and frightening that, on arriving at work, she immediately told a trusted, elderly colleague about it. She reacted very emotionally, assuring Lana that this dream was a prophetic one and that it could be a sign of big changes in her personal life.

At that moment, Lana was still recovering from her divorce with no trace of a new relationship. She was immersed in her work; it served as an excellent distraction. But she kept in mind the words of her colleague.

A sign of big changes in my personal life… What if it's true?

Lana began awaiting a miracle...

***

'She is awaiting a miracle!' Lily shouted. 'She is ready for a new relationship! Do you hear, Nicky? We need to organise something! Do you have anyone in mind?'

'I'm an angel, not a matchmaker,' Nicky muttered.

'Don't be lazy, Nicky! Use your brains! She is already on her way home and hopes for a miracle. We must not let her down!'

'Okay,' Nicky replied reluctantly, 'I have one guy.' And Nicky began listing, in a monotone: 'Thirty-five years old, single, handsome, earns decent money. His mother has been trying to marry him off for several years and uses every opportunity to do so. On the train, she recently met a friend of Lana's mother, and asked if she knew any good single women.'

'And what did she answer?' Lily asked, hopefully.

'She mentioned Tina, Lana's sister...'

***

Lana arrived at her mother's apartment and rang the doorbell. Her heart was pounding wildly, and the thought was revolving in her head: *If this dream really is prophetic, my mother will open the door and tell me news that will radically change my life!*

The door flew open, and her mother's first words were: 'Lana! I have such startling news for you!' She began talking about the phone call from her friend about a woman she met on the train and about arranging meeting between her son and… Tina.

Lana's eyes dimmed a little, but she thought, *Well, big changes in my sister's life can probably be seen as big changes in my life. The dream really was prophetic!*

***

The whole family went to meet the prospective groom: Tina, Mother, Lana, and Freeda.

The man's mother spoke nonstop, managing to tell all her love stories and all about the two famous people she had met in her life, all within an hour. The man, though, sat silently, blinking often.

Tina and mum listened politely, drank champagne and smiled. Lana did not sit down even for a moment, though, as her super-energetic toddler demanded a lot of attention.

***

'Mummy's boy is a big softie, but you will not get bored with his mother!'

Lana said to her sister as they returned home, laughing loudly.

At that moment the phone rang. It was a call from the "big softie's" mother who said her son would like to invite… Lana… on a date!

⁂

The marriage was held eight months later. Lana was a very beautiful bride. She danced a lot and sang karaoke at the reception:

> You got married somehow once
> Being jinxed by dark black eyes
> But you did not get nervous:
> Started getting used to those…yeah…

The marriage certificate was replaced by a divorce document a year later, but Lana was sure that the main wedding in her life was still ahead.

Chapter 9: Red Dress

Lana studied English all her life: first at school, then at university, and later attending various courses. She was preparing to work for a large international company, where knowledge of the language would, undoubtably, be necessary.

One of the courses she attended included English language songs. Lana did not like this module. She never understood the meaning of these songs and did not really try but, then, in one lesson, Eric Clapton's song 'Wonderful Tonight' captured her soul completely.

The class sang slowly, robotically, and without feeling. Lana looked around shocked and just could not fathom how they didn't catch, didn't understand, didn't *feel* this beautiful song!

She sang along, closing her eyes and imagining herself in the place of this beautiful woman. In her dreams she was wearing a long red dress and *he* was next to her – an English-speaking man who looked at her with love and delight.

***

'It seems she's started dreaming... a lot,' Lily sighed. *'What have you got there? Can't you hurry things along?'*

'No, Lily – HE isn't ready yet! He needs another ten years...' Nicky replied sadly.

'What can we do?'

'Let her take care of her studies, her career – oh, and raising her child. She has a lot to do, yet!' Nicky answered. 'But, she will meet HIM and will be surprised to learn that HE also loves this song! And there will be a red dress... but not for ten years.'

★★★

Lana cut her long hair and dyed it light. Along with the long hair, the men disappeared from her life.

The following years were busy. Lana built a successful career, finished an internationally recognised professional qualification, started tutoring high level courses, bought a luxury apartment and an expensive car, continued raising her daughter... But deep down she felt that something important was still missing in her life.

Part II - Success

Chapter 10: Lecturer

Lana was rapidly climbing the career ladder, having started with small firms, and gradually progressed to large organisations. She would join a company, stay there for several years, improve systems, train the staff, make friends, and move on to the next one to repeat this cycle.

At first, women perceived her with apprehension. What was such a young and beautiful lady doing in this position? Were there not more interesting things to do? But, gradually, youth and beauty became second to experience and professionalism.

Lana believed she was very lucky with her career choice. While others considered the profession of accountancy boring and uninteresting, Lana found it amazing, admiring the magic of numbers, and beautiful accounting reports and tax returns.

The results of her work were highly appreciated, internally and externally. A tax inspector once referred the accounting system developed by Lana to the Ministry of Finance, which was the highest praise he could offer.

Colleagues light-heartedly joked that Lana did not look like a proper accountant. They argued 'A real accountant must wear glasses and be angry!' Lana was the complete opposite of this image.

At some point, though, Lana realised that the accounting world was not standing still, and the knowledge gained at university was no longer enough to provide further growth. Without hesitation, she decided to improve her skills and complete a prestigious international accounting qualification.

Classes were held in the evenings after a hard workday, but Lana rushed straight there – eager for new knowledge!

She listened to each tutor's every word, in all courses but one. There was one subject that she would have liked to present in a different way. Lana corrected the lectures in her mind and imagined herself standing at the blackboard in the place of the tutor.

I would have explained this topic differently, much more easily. Here, I would give an example, like…

***

'*She is lost in dreams!*' Nicky snapped.

'*But, I like this!*' Lily said. '*She would be a good tutor.*'

'*Won't it be too much for her?*'

'I am sure she can manage it all!' Lily confidently defending her ward.

***

After successfully passing exams and completing the qualification, of course, Lana did not stop there and immediately went on to further study.

At the very first lesson, a big surprise awaited her – she was asked to teach others, and in exactly the subject she had dreamed of.

She accepted the offer immediately! Lana didn't even ask how much she would be paid, if at all. She was even ready to work for free! But it turned out that this work was paid very well, which was an unexpected bonus.

***

Lana had to prepare for the lectures at night because she was studying at the same time, working towards the next level. Sometimes she went to bed long after midnight and had to get up at six in the morning to take Freeda to school.

But she did not feel tired; she enjoyed everything she was doing.

She approached the preparation of her lectures creatively, trying to make them interesting with elements of competition. She realised that her students were accountants, like her, who came to classes tired after a hard day at work. She really wanted to make their life a bit easier.

The very first tests showed impressive results — almost all the trainees passed their exams in Lana's subject at the first attempt. She was even invited by course graduates to a restaurant. The students sat Lana at the head of the table, handed over a large bouquet of flowers and, one by one, began announcing their exam results – all of which were near the highest possible marks! Lana was incredibly happy!

Of course, not everything went so smoothly. There was one topic in the course that Lana did not relate to at all — the time value of money. She studied it thoroughly, so as to present it to the students as clearly as possible. It took her some time to fully understand the topic, but her explanation was a great success and Lana's trainees did calculations simply and easily.

One day she came to the class, having mistakenly picked up notes from the previous lecture. Lana had to deploy all her memory reserves and worked heroically at the blackboard for three hours. It became her recurring nightmare!

All in all, the classes were a success, and teaching became Lana's hobby for many years. Some of her students even became close friends.

Chapter 11: Palace

Lana settled into her new apartment, miraculously found that memorable hot summer. Her new home was spacious and bright, the windows providing an amazing view of the city. She began planning a grandiose renovation and even pictured her living room with a large sofa between two windows. Even though there was only one window in the actual room, she persistently saw her living room with two windows. *We will probably have to remove the wall between the living room and the kitchen to make the second window,* she told herself.

A colleague had once shared his impression of an apartment of a wealthy friend: "High ceilings, huge windows, marble floors, columns..." Thinking on this, Lana realised she no longer wanted to renovate her apartment. In fact, she didn't even want to live in this apartment. She wanted a new apartment with high ceilings, large windows, columns, and marble floors.

***

At that moment, the air filled with sparkling stars and the gentle sound of flattering angels' wings.

'Oh, how I love miracles!' Lily exclaimed. 'Why are people afraid to dream, leaving us without work?'

'But some of them dream too much,' Nicky answered disapprovingly, nodding his head towards Lana. 'Sometimes there is no time to even watch football!' (He had recently become an ardent supporter of London team The Arsenal.)

'Don't be lazy, Nicky!' Lily said. 'You are our expert in magical financial transactions! So do your work!'

***

Within a few months, Lana signed a contract to purchase of a different apartment – one with high ceilings and large windows. Later, marble floors, columns and, of course, a large sofa appeared between the two living room windows.

Friends of Lana's daughter were delighted.

'Freeda, you live in a palace!'

But Freeda didn't care. She didn't like anything her mother did.

Chapter 12: The Kiss

From early childhood, Lana showed a love of artists painting. Even though no one in the family was fond of art, there were several books about artists in the home library. Lana was attracted to these like a magnet. She read them repeatedly and knew all the titles illustrations by heart.

Lana's interest in famous painters grew in adulthood after reading the book, *Lust for Life*, about Vincent Van Gogh. Then she read *Torment and Joy* about the life of Michelangelo, *The Moon and Sixpence* about Paul Gauguin, and on and on...

Lana discovered more and more artists and quickly had her favourites. Among the Impressionists, she especially singled out Renoir, impressed by his love of life. The magnificent portraits of Hans Holbein, the court painter of the English king, Henry VIII, she began to take an interest in British history.

'Henry VIII was married six times! Two of his wives, Anne Boleyn, and her cousin Catherine Howard, ended their lives on the guillotine. The king dreamed of an heir, and the third wife, Jane Seymour, bore him a son but died soon after giving birth. The fourth wife, Anna of Cleves, was immortalized by Hans Holbein in a magnificent portrait, but the king did not

35

appreciate her beauty, calling her "a Flanders mare", and insisted on divorce.' Lana loved sharing newly acquired knowledge with her daughter.

Freeda listened to her mother's stories without enthusiasm and only once, instead of reading before going to bed, agreed to listen to the story of Michelangelo's life and view his paintings.

'One day, we will go to the Vatican and see the ceiling of the Sistine Chapel with our own eyes!' Lana finished her story.

'Va-ti-can,' Lily immediately wrote it down in her notebook, drawing out the syllables.

Lana really wanted to instil a love of painting in her daughter, or at least give her some knowledge and a place to begin, but Freeda resisted. So, Lana devised another approach; she decided to help Freeda with her homework for art class.

'What were you asked to draw this time?' she enquired of her daughter.

'I don't remember… Maybe a still life?' Freeda answered, reluctantly.

Lana found a favourite example from Paul Cézanne and helped Freeda sketch it, while telling her a story about the painting and the artist.

The next time, having received an assignment to paint an autumn landscape, Freeda redrew Gustav Klimt's *Birch Grove* with her mother's help.

This way Lana introduced Freeda to a new artist and a new painting every week. Lana conscientiously prepared for joint drawing lessons, each time telling her daughter something interesting and memorable. But Lana's dream was to see all these paintings with her own eyes, visiting the most famous art galleries in the world.

'What's on our list?' Lily asked. 'The Louvre in Paris, Madrid's Museo del Prado, The Uffizi in Florence, London's National Gallery... We must start somewhere! Let's start with somewhere closer – The Hermitage...'

'What if we go to St. Petersburg to visit Aunt Louise?' Lana offered, unexpectedly. Freeda happily agreed, Louise was her beloved relative. The main thing Lana expected from this trip was seeing The Hermitage Museum's the magnificent collection of Impressionists.

They went to The Hermitage on the first day of their visit. However, Lana did not get to see paintings of the famous French artists that day. The museum was so expansive that, when they finally got to the halls of the Impressionists, poor Freeda could not stand it, needing a break, some food and the facilities. Lana was terribly upset, but the very next day, after some hours at beautiful Peterhof Palace, Freeda kindly offered to visit the Hermitage again.

'Let's quickly see your impressionists and leave right away!' she said.

But they didn't manage to leave right away, because they accidentally ended up in the hall of Henri Matisse on the way back. Lana had heard about this artist but was completely unfamiliar with his work. Seeing the huge composition, *The Dance*, she simply was lost for words. Three main colours: red, blue, and green. Five dancing figures. That's all there was — but it held so much more! There was something about the painting that Lana simply couldn't take her eyes from. Even Freeda stood quietly beside her, gazing with admiration at the breath-taking canvas.

* * *

'Let's go to a book shop and buy something about Matisse,' Louise suggested, after hearing the enthusiastic story about the magnificent painting.

While Lana was choosing books about artists, her beloved aunt stood nearby, also perusing a book. *Klimt*, Lana noted to herself, glancing out the corner of her eye at the book in Louise's hands, which suddenly fell open at one of the pages.

'Oh, *The Kiss*! I really love this picture,' Lana said.

'What? What did you say? What is it called?' Louise asked, agitated.

'*The Kiss* is one of Gustav Klimt's masterpieces,' Lana told her.

'A masterpiece?' Louise seemed tense.

'Yes, a masterpiece. What's the matter? Why are you so nervous?' Lana asked.

'I'll tell you at home,' Louise snapped. They quickly paid for their chosen books and rushed out.

At home, Louise lifted a strange picture off the kitchen wall. It was in a beautiful wooden frame with a pattern similar to the famous Klimt style, and she told Lana a story about it.

By working all her life as a librarian in a boarding school for children with disabilities, Louise accidentally established herself among her loved ones as a great intellectual and connoisseur of art. When one of the nieces gave her a small reproduction of Klimt's *The Kiss* in a beautiful wooden frame and said, 'I'm sure you will appreciate it!', Louise had no choice but to pretend that she knew it and loved the gift.

Arriving home, she studied the picture for a long time, pondering how to hang it. She tried with the kissing people on their backs, put them on their knees, on their stomachs; but, in every position, in her opinion, the picture looked strange. Then she pulled the incomprehensible picture from the frame and instead inserted a photograph of her deceased husband, which after a while was also removed from the frame and replaced by an unpretentious picture of a sailing ship.

Quietly amused at Louise's ignorance, Lana immediately decided to restore justice and return the *The Kiss* to its rightful place! But, they could not find the original picture. 'I probably threw it away,' Louise admitted, blushing.

Then Lana took the new book about Klimt and cut out a fragment of the page with *The Kiss,* so that it fit into the frame.

'Can you see what I preferred to this masterpiece?' Louise asked timidly before Lana changed the pictures.

'Frame size: ten by fifteen. The price: Eighteen rubles,' Lana read the caption under the picture, looked at Louise in amazement, and they burst into laughter.

'What are you laughing at? Tell me!' Freeda asked.

They shared the story and Louise then phoned her friends, telling them and laughing again.

***

After some time, Louise's house was filled with things associated with Klimt: cups, books, pictures. Not only did she buy these for herself, but she also gave them to her friends, who in turn passed on knowledge about the great Austrian artist to the next generations – their children and grandchildren.

'Gustav Klimt, *The Three Ages of Woman*,' the granddaughter of one of Louise's friends said confidently, seeing a reproduction on the cover of a mathematics teacher's diary. The teacher was so impressed by the erudition of this C-student, this simple statement immediately affected her grades in algebra and geometry, making them slightly higher.

Thanks to this story, Freeda also remembered the painting very well.

'Oh, it's your *Kiss*,' she said casually to Lana, seeing a reproduction at a local McDonald's.

'It's so good that you know that – hundreds of children pass this picture every day and have no idea what it is!' Lana said, with pride.

Chapter 13: We Did Not Pay for That!

Although Lana was born in the USSR, like millions of other Soviet children, she was christened in church. Parents often adhered to religious tradition, while children were indoctrinated at school that the Lord Almighty did not exist (this was drilled into everyone) and were told horrific stories about the religious rituals of believers.

As a result, Lana the child sarcastically questioned her grandmother's beliefs, as she said the Lord's Prayer every night before going to bed.

'Granny, do you really think God exists?' Lana asked laughingly.

'God does not necessarily mean God as described in the Bible, but there is some being beyond our understanding,' the grandmother answered. She wrote the Lord's Prayer on a piece of paper and gave it to her granddaughter.

Lana kept this piece of paper, but it was left untouched for several years. Then, one day, her classmate did not stand when the lecturer entered the theatre, as was the usual custom. He said that, for him, this custom was reserved for morning prayer. In joking reply, the tutor asked him to stand up and say the Lord's Prayer. Imagine the amazement when he got up and said the whole prayer without the slightest hesitation!

On that very day Lana again found the piece of paper with the prayer written by her grandmother and learned it by heart. From that moment on, saying the prayer became part of her daily routine.

She also began to occasionally attend church. Only occasionally, because she didn't feel very comfortable there. She did not know how to behave correctly and which icon to light candles at, fearing she might confuse 'for health' with 'at peace'. She also really did not like that no one was allowed to sit in Orthodox churches.

In contrast, she felt natural and at home in Catholic and Protestant churches. She loved to go there, sit down and think – sometimes just dream. Receiving an invitation to a charity concert of organ music in the local Lutheran Church brought much happiness and excitement! She would take Freeda and invited her friend Lucy with her daughter, Asya, who was the same age as Freeda.

***

Asya slept calmly for almost the entire concert, not bothering anyone, but Freeda was restless.

'How much longer?' she pleaded, incessantly.

Lana gave her a program and asked her to follow the running order. After each composition, Freeda recounted how many "songs" were left, loudly announcing it to everyone, and making it difficult for anyone to peacefully enjoy the music.

Lana felt awkward, aware of those sitting around her. To calm her daughter, she promised that they would all go somewhere for dinner after the concert if Freeda behaved quietly. Hearing the word "food", Asya awoke and both girls began counting the number of "songs" remaining to the end of the performance in a loud whisper.

When the last piece was complete and applause given, it was announced another composition would be played as an encore. Freeda loudly declared, 'We did not pay for that!'

This phrase became firmly established in the family lexicon and was used many times and in several languages, including English!

***

After the concert, they went to a small and cosy restaurant, not far from the church. During dinner, Freeda declared the concert terrible, but Asya disagreed and said she had really enjoyed it, especially the first part...

Chapter 14: She Is The One!

'I don't want to work here anymore!' Lana exclaimed, looking at the computer screen. This was her first experience working for an international company where she was selected from a large number of applicants.

To tell the truth, Lana had prepared thoroughly for the interview for this position. She rehearsed her speech repeatedly in English and accurately foresaw the questions so that she had answers prepared in advance.

But now, she realised it was not at all that she had dreamed of; the workload was heavy and tedious.

***

'Nicky, have you finished watching football yet? Just take one moment, please. Maybe you have something for her?' Lily asked.

'Well,' Nicky muttered, *'there is a big international oil company. They need such... a star.'*

***

The very next moment, Lana started browsing a specialist website and saw a vacancy at an international oil company that had been outstanding for a long time. 'A chief accountant with knowledge of English and IFRS is required...' she read.

45

This is exactly what I am looking for! Lana thought and immediately sent her CV.

***

'Well, what do you think?' the HR manager asked the CEO after the interview with Lana.

By this time, they had already interviewed a huge number of candidates, and in each case, the CEO found something that did not suit him; not enough experience, knowledge, confidence, or even just that their nails looked not well-groomed. All boxes were ticked by Lana; from her knowledge and experience to her perfect manicure.

He leaned against the back of his chair and said, slowly, 'I think, maybe, she is the one.'

'She's definitely the one!' HR manager responded. 'It's not even worth looking further!'

***

So that's why I've been studying English all my life, Lana thought after getting the job in this prestigious international company.

Lana loved everything new, and the large volume of work did not frighten her at all. Many years ago, while still quite young, she was selected for the position of chief accountant at one of Ukraine's largest national holdings and she had to decide whether to accept the role. It was a huge manufacturing company and she felt, at that time, that she did not have enough experience. She had asked herself (and the Universe); *Will I be able to cope?* She received the answer: *If you are afraid now, what will happen in ten or fifteen years?* She immediately accepted the offer and, of course, took everything in her stride.

This new role within the oil company provided Lana with a series of impressive achievements, firstly by introducing the most modern accounting software available. Employees of the software developer's company watched in amazement as Lana worked selflessly, and practically alone, through the new version of this computer software.

'You are our special customer!' they said, hurrying to assist with her first support call.

Lana was also always lucky with her supporting team; all her accountants were smart, responsible, and very positive towards their boss.

'We do everything right and pay taxes honestly. Do we really need this?' Lana once complained to her colleague after yet another unfair tax inspection.

'You're doing everything right,' her colleague replied. 'So, keep doing it and do not pay attention to anyone!'

Lana couldn't do it any other way. She always tried to do everything very well, sparing no time or effort to achieve accuracy and precision. Of course, small setbacks occasionally arose, but Lana never got hung up on them. She quickly analysed the situation not to make the same mistakes in the future, and immediately got it out of her head. On the other hand, she rejoiced at her successes and achievements, reliving them often, and focusing on the happy memories.

'Think well, do well and all will be well!' was Lana's principal phrase. And she really felt very, very happy!

Chapter 15: "Sunrise, Sunset..."

Throughout her childhood, Lana dreamed of taking up ballroom dancing, but her parents preferred she learn to play the piano. An expensive instrument was bought, and Lana's years of torment began.

Lana hated music lessons. She did not miss classes but did everything to avoid preparing for them. The day before the lesson, she used to open the piano, put music on it, then go for a walk with her friends.

When her parents returned home from work, they would ask, 'Lana, were you preparing for music class?' Lana would point demonstratively, her hand at the open piano and reply, indignantly, 'Of course, I did! Don't you see?'

Her other favourite trick was to start preparing for a music lesson while her parents were watching an interesting movie on TV. Lana rattled deliberately loudly on the keys, pressing the forte pedal with all her might until her father stopped her by saying, 'Lana, it seems to me that you are ready for the lesson.' Obediently, she would remove the music, put the piano lid down and sit with her parents in front of the TV.

***

Now settled in her new job, Lana decided to realise her unfulfilled childhood dream via her daughter – enrolling her in ballroom dancing school. Freeda hated it and tried to persuade her mother to enrol her in piano lessons, but Lana was adamant.

Freeda was not going to give up, and once even managed to miss a whole month of classes, assuring her mother that they had not yet started. The lie was revealed in a casual phone conversation with the mother of one of her classmates. By this time, Freeda's dancing partner had already been paired with another, and the little liar had to make great efforts to bring him back.

Lana, on the other hand, treated her daughter's dancing lessons with great responsibility; expensive ball gowns were bought and sewn, various competitions paid for. Dancing, itself, was an expensive pleasure. But Lana did not regret the spending to make her childhood dream come true. In her dreams, she saw her daughter winning international tournaments! Though Freeda only sometimes became the winner of small local contests, Lana never stopped dreaming.

***

'*I feel sorry for this silly-billy: she has been doing her best for her daughter, but Freeda doesn't care!*' Nicky said.

He turned to Lily.

'*Maybe you can arrange something?*'

'*It's not that easy,*' Lily replied. '*Freeda is one of a kind! But I'll do my best.*'

***

Quite unexpectedly, Freeda and her dance partner, Denis, were chosen to prepare a routine for a recital of the dancing school ensemble. Only the best and most talented dancers received this honour. Lana was surprised, but very happy. Inspired, she set to work creating a routine.

The chosen set for the performance was a slow waltz — Lana's least favourite dance of the standard program.

Never mind, we will find a melody and stage such a spectacle that it will be the best dance of the concert!

The first challenge was to choose the music. For many long nights, Lana listened to numerous slow waltzes, saving the best ones, and listening to those over and over. She wanted to find a melody that would capture the audience from the very first notes and transport them to the magical world of dance. But each piece had something which did not feel quite right.

As the nights of listening to piece after piece continued, Lana was becoming desperate. She was going to bed as morning emerged after one lengthy session, when suddenly, out of the blue, the magic voice of Perry Como drifted into her brain: 'Sunrise, sunset, sunrise, sunset...'

This was exactly what she was looking for!

Lana immediately woke her mother and asked her to listen to the song. Mum, surprisingly not resisting, put on headphones, closed her eyes, and agreed after the very first chords. 'Perfect!'

The next challenge was choreography. None of the school dance teachers approved of the choice of music. Everyone agreed the melody was very difficult for such young dancers. But Lana didn't give up, and she had no doubt that the children would manage well.

The task of choreography was solved when a young dance teacher from another city suddenly appeared, happily staging the dance.

Thus, the dance was ready, and Lana was looking forward to the recital.

★★★

Serendipitously, Lana and her family got the best seats in the auditorium. She took her seat in the 'Royal Box' and waited impatiently for her daughter's performance.

Finally, the air began to fill with the magical music and the audience was captivated by the beautiful dance. Everyone was projected into a mystical world!

Lana now knew every element of the composition by heart and, looking at the children floating across the stage, she did not notice any mistakes. She simply enjoyed their magnificent waltz, tears of happiness rolling down her cheeks. It was the feeling she had dreamed of for so long!

When the dance was over, the audience burst into applause and Freeda and Denis received a huge number of congratulations and rave reviews after the recital. Beyond any doubt, it was the best dance of the concert.

***

'Sunrise, Sunset' became the most memorable and beautiful event in Freeda's dance career. After that, Lana and her mum revisited the recording of the dance many times, experiencing the same happy emotions over and over.

Meanwhile, Freeda took refuge in her bedroom, shutting the room door firmly, plugging headphones in and turning her own music up.

'I hate "Sunrise, Sunset"!'

Chapter 16: Diamonds

I'm almost forty, and I have no diamonds, Lana thought.

Her friend, Lucy had a husband who gave her diamonds on every wedding anniversary, but Lana didn't have a husband or diamonds.

I should at least buy some, myself! she decided.

At that time, Lana had just finished giving a series of lectures and had enough to purchase diamond jewellery, even if the diamonds would be very small. She decided to make the purchase the following Saturday, as Freeda had a ballroom dancing competition on the Sunday after.

***

Lana didn't like leaving things until the last minute, so the first thing she did early Saturday morning was to prepare Freeda's ballgown, intending to go to the jewellery store after.

As she slowly ironed the dress, Lana pictured how gorgeous she would look at her daughter's competition in her new diamond earrings. This distraction led to a huge burnt hole in the ball gown (*Oh, my God!*), and it was irreparable. Forfeiting was not an option, as there were hopes of some success at the event.

Freeda was looking at Lana with terror in her eyes, not understanding how such an important task as ironing was entrusted to such an irresponsible woman like her mother, who only knew how to deal with her laptop! Granny was much better at things like this!

'That's okay, no problem!' Lana said, confidently. 'We'll buy a new gown!'

Despite her bravado, Freeda and her grandmother knew it was almost impossible to find a new dress of the right size and style less than a day before the competition, but they began getting ready. Lana threw the wad of cash earned from her lectures into her handbag, promising herself that diamonds would wait.

It was a lengthy shopping trip but, thankfully, in the very last store, they managed to find what they were looking for – a gorgeous, pale pink, whalebone dress of the right size, and at a price much cheaper than Lana was prepared for.

The girls were so happy!

At the register, Lana quickly plucked the required amount from the wad of notes and tossed the rest back into her handbag.

***

At this moment, out of nowhere, Nicky appeared and said, 'Let's check how she reacts!'

In an instant, he had moved the money into an unused and secret pocket of Lana's mother's handbag.

***

Satisfied and happy, the girls went to the jewellery store, but Lana discovered there was no money in her handbag! She checked everything several times, panicking, then she asked her mother to check her handbag, just in case. There was no money anywhere!

On the way home, they tried to think when the money could have been stolen, but Lana was pragmatic.

Well, you were ready to spend at all on a dress...

Her mood immediately improved – she even smiled.

***

'Did you hear, Nicky? She passed your test! It's time to give the money back and let her buy diamonds after all. She deserves it!' Lily cried.

'Yes, she did,' Nicky agreed. 'But it's not time yet. I've prepared something else for her...'

***

Over a cup of coffee at home, Lana told her mother that, though she was glad Freeda now had a dress, she was disappointed not to be able to buy herself a piece of diamond jewellery. Her mother suggested they go look to see if they could get something with small diamonds with the money not spent on Freeda, so they gathered their remaining savings and went back to the jewellery store.

After hearing the story of the stolen money, the store manager gave Lana such a discount that she bought everything she wanted with the smaller amount available.

***

The next day was full of miracles!

First, Lana's mother said that she had a dream where the stolen money was returned. And indeed, within a half an hour, the money was found in the secret pocket, which they had never even noticed before.

Most importantly, though, Freeda and her partner won gold medals in both programs of the ballroom competition! Their coach kept repeating, 'I don't understand how they did it. This is some kind of miracle!'

'You haven't seen miracles yet!' said Nicky, bristling with pride.

Chapter 17: Losing Leonard

Over the next weeks, Freeda persistently tried to persuade Lana to learn to drive and buy a car. At school, every day she was seeing more and more mothers driving, while her mum still took public transport. Lana simply didn't have the time to learn to drive, or the money to buy a car.

One day, Lana and Freeda were returning home on the tram from a friend's birthday. On route, Freeda suggested they visit a shopping centre. Lana, reluctantly, agreed.

'Sit here!' Freeda demanded and sat Lana at a child's car simulator, starting the game.

'Well, did you enjoy it?' she asked, after the virtual ride.

'Well… so-so,' Lana said hesitantly.

'Oh, I see,' Freeda screeched. 'We will take the tram until you retire!' Lana looked at Freeda in amazement.

She's right!

***

Lily happily waved her little wings and said, 'Have you heard, Nicky? She wants to drive! I can already imagine her driving a beautiful silver car!'

'Well, what's so exciting about that?' Nicky replied. 'It's normal for women in England to drive – nobody thinks anything of it.'

***

Within a month, Lana began driving lessons — conveniently just five minutes' walk from her office and the schedule matched perfectly with her lectures.

The driving coach was a handsome young man named Leonard, who looked ten years younger than Lana. He seemed to treat her differently from the other students, often looking at her and smiling.

***

'He's staring at her,' Nicky said, *'because she's asking stupid questions all the time.'*

'It's not that at all!' Lily cried. *'He's obviously fallen in love with her!'*

***

Lana's friend — who was on the same course — saw it the same way and told Lana.

Boring courses suddenly became exciting events. Lana looked forward to each session, noticing the coach's eyes made her feel cheerful and happy.

'You need to do something!' her friend said. 'He's indecisive, you need to push him. We'll stay after class for practice tests next time, to give him a chance to ask you out on a date.'

60

By now Lana had grown her hair long again and dyed it red. She was very conscientious about preparing for the next class; bright makeup, a beautiful dress, and her favourite Givenchy perfume.

But then something went wrong.

After class, while the girls were enthusiastically doing practice tests on the computer, Leonard and his fellow teachers loudly rattled their keys, making it clear that they had other plans for this evening, and it was time for the girls to finish.

***

'We are losing Leonard! We are losing Leonard!' her friend cried after the door of the driving school slammed behind them. 'We urgently need a Plan B!'

But this "love story" finished before it began, and it was already completely unimportant for Lana.

Chapter 18: Marisa

Lana finally passed her driving test a few days before her fortieth birthday. The next question was which car to buy, and when. Opinions were divided. Some said she should buy immediately, while the driving lessons were still fresh in her mind. Others advised waiting until spring when the snow and ice passed. Lana was undecided and did not know which was the best advice.

'You should take my advice,' Nicky said. *'You need to buy a car now, not wait for spring!'*
But it goes without saying that Lana didn't hear him.

During a taxi ride to a lecture the next day, she discussed the issue with the driver, giving strong arguments that she was still an inexperienced driver, and it would be safer for her and for others to wait until spring.
Throughout the journey the driver agreed, but when Lana got out of the car — feeling relieved that the decision had finally been made — the taxi door opened and the driver shouted, 'But actually, you should buy it now!'

***

Lana's colleague, Alex, was a motorsport enthusiast who loved speed and motorbikes, and he offered to help her choose a car. He helped her do a few test drives, directing her towards cool sports cars.

Other opinions were also considered. For example, Freeda believed the car had to be black. Lana's mother came to the rescue, saying that dirt and dust were very visible on a black surface, and this, of course, was impractical.

(Some might doubt this, but proof arrived when a tired and stressed woman in a car park was seen writing in thick dirt on her husband car with her finger: "Clean me". Grandma looked at her sceptical granddaughter: 'You see? I told you!' So ended any interest in black cars.)

Lana was struck and her heart began to pound when she set eyes on a brand-new silver Toyota Corolla.

That's it! I want this one and only this one! It's mine!

Unfortunately, the car was already booked by another customer, so Lana was offered the same model in red with many year-end incentives. She was deeply upset but decided not to purchase the red model.

63

***

'Nicky, can you do something for her?' Lily asked. *'Look, she just fell in love with this car! She doesn't sleep at night and only talks about it over and over!'*

'All right,' Nicky said. *'I'll carry out some complicated financial transaction for her!'*

'You are so smart, Nicky!'

Nicky smiled contentedly, as Lily did not often indulge him with compliments.

***

The next day, the phone rang at Lana's office. A clerk at the Toyota showroom called and said that the buyer of the silver model would not be able to pay the second part of the payment on time and was therefore happy to exchange the silver model for the red one – but the silver model had no incentives: no set of winter tyres, no TV set, no T-shirt, calendar, cup, and pen.

Though thrilled, Lana was firm that she needed all or nothing, and hung up. She regretted it immediately!

But within ten minutes, the dealer called again and confirmed that all promotional gifts would be included as well.

***

'Can you imagine? They gave me winter tyres, a TV set, a T-shirt, a cup, a pen...' Lana excitedly told her cousin on the telephone.

He chuckled, 'It feels like you are happier about the pen and cup than the car!'

This is how the beautiful silver Toyota appeared in Lana's life. She was named Marisa.

Chapter 19: Python Ate Five Rabbits

Gorgeous, thought Lana, looking in the mirror of the fitting room. She had dashed to the nearest store during her lunch break and saw this beautiful outfit: shorts and matching top, figure hugging, mainly olive-coloured, with imitation python pattern.

In high-heels Lana looked awesome in this python set, although she had to pull her tummy in a little.

I will buy it!

***

'Nicky, don't you think she needs a hint that it's time to start going to the gym? HE is about to appear in her life, but she doesn't seem ready. Just look at her stomach!' Lily said.

'You women only think about unimportant things,' Nicky replied. 'You always think about irrelevancies! I need to focus on important matters – Arsenal is losing to Liverpool!'

***

Arriving home, Lana quickly changed into new clothes and proudly called for Freeda. To demonstrate the new outfit in all its glory, she went to the middle of the room, took the pose of a Victoria's Secret model, and stood waiting for compliments.

Freeda glanced at her mother out of the corner of her eye and said, 'Ah! The python ate five rabbits!'

Lana had not anticipated a compliment like that! She looked in the mirror and, instead of a slender model, suddenly saw a woman with a protruding stomach!

* * *

"...twelve, thirteen, fourteen, fifteen..." counted Lily, fluttering over Lana doing abdominal exercises in the gym the very next day.

Chapter 20: Dating Site

Lana's close friend Ana, who was living abroad, came to Odessa. Lana proudly dragged her to her home to show off her achievements.

First, Lana walked her friend through her luxurious apartment, stopping at each notable sight and sharing the story of every tiny feature. Lana continued to share her all achievements as they entered the kitchen, where there were glasses filled with sparkling wine: career, international qualifications, tutoring, her daughter's successes… Lana talked and talked and could not stop. She had so much to say!

Ana was quiet, sipping wine and smiling politely at her stories. Then she interrupted with a question, 'Apartment, work, tutoring, daughter… All very good. But what about your personal life?'

Lana was taken aback; she had no immediate answer. She collected her thoughts and started defending.

'Well, firstly, there is no time for dating in my busy schedule. Even if I found time, where could I meet a man? I no longer go to nightclubs, going to a restaurant alone would be very odd, and at parties and birthdays that I get invited to, there are no single men.'

To Lana these arguments seemed rigorous enough for the topic to be closed, but Ana continued.

'What about dating sites?'

'Oh, no! Lana responded. 'Not for me! There are only idiots and sex maniacs on these sites...'

'How do you know? Have you ever tried?' her friend asked.

'No, I haven't, but... I know,' Lana answered, suddenly hesitant.

'Try it!' said Ana. Taking a scrap of paper, she wrote the address of a dating site and placed it on the kitchen shelf.

The conversation reverted to Lana's comfort zone, and she would have forgotten about her friend's question forever, were it not for her stumbling across this piece of paper when she reorganised her kitchen a couple of weeks later...

Chapter 21: 'Hi!'

Whilst cleaning up the kitchen in the lead up to Christmas, Lana found a piece of paper with the address of a dating site written on it. She glanced at it, froze for a moment, then crumpled it and was about to throw it into the rubbish bin, but...

...*Lily and Nicky appeared from nowhere and grabbed Lana's hand with all their might.*
'Hold tight, Nicky!' Lily shouted.
'I'm doing the best I can,' Nicky grumbled back. 'Damn, she is strong! That work at the gym is paying off.'

At that moment, Lana's hand stopped. She smoothed the crumpled piece of paper, took it in both hands, looked at it carefully and said, 'Why not?'

"Ooh..." Lily and Nicky breathed out at the same time, wiping the sweat from their brow.

Lana moved to her computer and quickly typed in the site's address. A few discoveries awaited her. First, none of the profiles looked like idiots or sex maniacs.
They look normal...
Then she decided to look at the profiles of women and what she saw just amazed her: passionate, sexy women of

various ages, some very beautiful and others not so. Profiles with deep cleavage, partially closed, suggestive glances and pouting lips peered at her. It seemed to Lana that they were trying to set traps for men – she could almost hear their sighs!

Stunned, Lana approached the mirror, bared her shoulder, and tried her most passionate look.

Yeah, you won't get far with such a serious accountant's appearance!

She uploaded her most ordinary photos — having cut Freeda from them — with no expectation of success.

After all, look at the competition!

To Lana's surprise, in the very first days, a Dutchman and a Swiss man approached her, persuading her to leave the site and use Skype and email for further communication. Over the following four months, the two entertained her, and even sent a bouquet of roses for her birthday. It was agreed that the Dutch man would come to Odessa in February, and she would meet the other in a tropical country in March.

* * *

'HE is finally ready!' Nicky reported.
'I get it!' Lily was ecstatic.

***

On December 30, mainly in curiosity, Lana decided to visit the dating site again. *I'll just take a quick look at what's going on…*

There were many old messages, and she was about to read through them, when a short new message arrived:

"Hi!" N. London

"Hi!" Lana answered – without a moment's hesitation.

Part III – Love

Chapter 22: It Is Him, or The Impossible Becomes Possible

Lana knew exactly what kind of man she wanted to meet. There were only two conditions: he must be an Englishman or an American (because Lana did not want to learn another foreign language) and he must not have children (since she really wanted her chosen one to become a true father for her daughter).

'No, not an American!' said Lana's mother. 'America is so far away!'

'I agree!' said Lily, watching from a corner.

'A man without children? At your age?' continued Mum. 'It's impossible!'

'Even the impossible becomes possible if you want it enough!' Lily chuckled.

The Dutchman more or less suited Lana's requirements; he spoke English well and had no children, since he had never been married. The Swiss man had three children. He was in the final stages of a long divorce process, but the chemistry was so good that Lana found him very fun and interesting, and she was looking forward to meeting him in March.

And what about our "Hi" from London? Lana quickly browsed his profile – there were no photos or personal story. She thought him mysterious and impossible, and continued active communication with her new friends from The Netherlands and Switzerland.

But the mysterious Englishman was persistent. His name was Neil, and he wrote every day; very delicately, politely, and pleasantly, showing sincere interest in her life.

At first this irritated Lana a little, as it distracted her from communicating with more important suitors. Sometimes she even answered brusquely. But Lana gradually realised she was impatiently waiting for the evening communication with this man. Her heart began to beat faster when that sweet "Hi" came from London in the evenings.

The others suddenly seemed intrusive and uninteresting to her. Lana was not even sure that she wanted to meet them.

'We need to cancel the proposed meetings urgently!' Lily said, giving Nicky instructions. *'I'll take the Dutchman, and you deal with the Swiss!'*

First, a message arrived that the Dutchman had to postpone his visit to a later date – he had suddenly lost a tooth and he could not come to a potential bride with a gap in his teeth.

Then the Swiss man wrote a very long and sad message. His wife decided to reconsider all the conditions for divorce, which meant further extension of the already long and painful process. Lana sympathized and agreed that this was not the best time to meet, that it would be sensible to wait.

Lana secretly glowed; this cleared the way for her to communicate with Neil!

He quickly became close and so dear to her.

Is it possible to fall in love with a person just by talking online, without ever meeting? What she felt for this man could not be called anything other than love.

They simply talked about nothing, almost every day, for hours, at every opportunity, and missed each other very much if they couldn't exchange messages even for one day (which was normally when Arsenal was playing away games).

But, I don't even know what he looks like!

Neil's dating page was still completely blank. At her request, he sent a photo of himself, accompanied by the comment: "Be prepared for disappointment."

When Lana saw his face, she just could not believe her eyes: this was the man she had seen in her dreams over the years, the man who spoke English. She also caught herself thinking there was a

75

resemblance to her first husband, Freeda's father, who had died suddenly a couple of years before.

Lana went to his funeral. His last common-law wife grieved over him, staying near the coffin. His various other partners were also present (there were quite a few of them!). However, the attention of most of those attending was on Lana. Everyone agreed that, of all his relationships, she was the best influence and that he was a different man with her – a kind man.

At the funeral service in the church, continuously brushing the hot wax off her hand from a melting candle, Lana felt forgiveness toward him and thanked him for her biggest treasure — their daughter, Freeda.

So, now, Lana knew what Neil looked like. What else? She knew he was an ardent fan of Arsenal football club, that he had a small real estate business, that he had been married for more than twenty years, but the love had passed, and the couple had decided to get divorced. They had no children.

Is this really HIM?

Lana could not believe her happiness; events were developing so quickly.

***

'Of course, it is HIM, silly woman! How much more proof do you need?' Nicky was frustrated.

'Nicky, I think it's time for a meeting on neutral territory – it's the obvious next step.' Lily said.

Chapter 23: The Blue Mosque, or First Meeting

A month after their first communication, Lana and Neil began to arrange a meeting on neutral territory. They agreed to meet in Istanbul, as it was easy for Lana to get there from Odessa.

The choice of meeting place seemed simple enough. But Lana found it strange that Neil suggested meeting during the work week – for her it was more logical to meet over a weekend. She would learn that his days off were forever reserved for the main hobby in his life, football.

Neil, very delicately, offered to pay for the trip and Lana graciously agreed. She carefully selected every item of clothing, so everything was prepared.

***

Lana arrived first, Neil's plane from London was due a few hours later. At the airport she was met by a driver and taken to the hotel — Neil had even taken care of that! Two separate hotel rooms were reserved in a small and cosy hotel located just a couple of minutes' walk from the famous Blue Mosque.

In order not to waste time, Lana booked a Turkish hammam and several excursions at the reception desk. Then she went to her room to wait as she didn't want to explore without Neil. She tried to read a book but couldn't concentrate as her heart was beating with excitement. So, she decided to go to the lobby and wait for Neil's arrival there.

The receptionist, sensing Lana's excitement, began a conversation, learning that this was their first meeting. Everything seemed so interesting to him, he began to look forward to Neil's arrival, too.

Then the door opened and a man who resembled Neil slowly entered the hotel. Passing Lana, he gave her a slight nod, as if to say 'Hello', and went to the front desk.

Maybe it's not him? Lana was puzzled. As she listened to his conversation, she heard his name clearly. Lana and the receptionist looked at each other in surprise: this was not the reaction they had anticipated!

Ever a hopeless dreamer, Lana had imagined a very emotional meeting with a hug – perhaps even a kiss. They had talked so much and already knew each other so well, that the meeting seemed to be a simple formality, the logical end of a virtual acquaintance and the beginning of a real relationship.

Neil later explained his behaviour: "I saw a woman even more beautiful than the photos. I wanted, so much, to run up immediately, hug and kiss her, but I was not sure if she wanted the same, so I gave her the opportunity to decide."

Having finished the check-in formalities, Neil suggested they go for a walk. Lana happily agreed, and the receptionist smiled and sighed with relief.

'May I take your hand?' Neil asked when they left the hotel.

'Sure!' Lana replied with a smile.

He confidently took her hand, interlocking their fingers.

'Oh, we don't hold hands like that,' Lana said and showed Neil her usual method of holding hands, then returned her hand back to the strong, English finger-lock.

When she kept her fingers interlocked with his, Neil thought with relief, *All will be well.*

It was a warm and sunny March day. They walked the streets of Istanbul, hand in hand, and chatted nonstop about nothing. They just talked and enjoyed every moment. Drivers of passing cars honked them with a smile, passers-by stopped them and paid compliments. Love was visible to the naked eye!

Later, there was dinner at a restaurant. In her bad English, she told him about her love of art and beautiful paintings, he told her he had 'a passing interest' in football. It turned out that football was a relevant topic to Lana, as one of her ex-boyfriends was a professional footballer and even played for one of the top Turkish clubs. But, when she got back to the hotel, Lana realised that she had not understood most of what Neil was saying. Her knowledge of English was worse than she thought, but it did not matter at all. She was happy – ecstatic!

It seemed only one hotel room was needed. But Neil went into his room each morning to unmake the bed, so the maids would think he was sleeping in his room and did not judge Lana. Lana laughed when she learned this, but she was so pleased.

My dear, old-fashioned Englishman! she thought with love and tenderness, *Chivalry is alive.*

Those days of continuous happiness flew by very quickly. Saying goodbye, they could not hold back their tears, but they knew for sure that this was only the beginning of a new life that both had dreamt of for so long.

***

'Lana!'

Someone loudly called her name in the check-in queue at Istanbul airport. It turned out to be a pupil of Lana's. On the plane, they sat side by side and throughout the journey the student praised Lana's outstanding teaching.

Just days before this would have made Lana incredibly happy – but now it did not seem very important. She only wanted to sit in silence, close her eyes and re-live all the wonderful moments of the magical meeting with Neil…

Chapter 24: Island of Happiness

The couple next met in London, with the main purpose of introducing Freeda to Neil. Lana was sure Neil would accept and love Freeda for herself, but the big question was how her capricious daughter would treat him.

'You have a better car,' Freeda said to Lana when she saw Neil's car. This turned out to be her only complaint, however Freeda accepted Neil immediately, as if she had known him forever.

As a great art lover, Lana also had big cultural plans for this trip to London. She had dreamed of visiting the National Gallery, so she could finally see the paintings of Hans Holbein, one of her favourite artists, first-hand. Neil was advised in advance of this, and all the other things on her list. Imagine her amazement when it turned out that the entire cultural tour was concentrated around Freeda's interests!

First, they went to an amusement park. Lana did not enjoy all the rides, but Freeda made them try them all, including the extreme ones – where she sat between her mother and Neil, clinging to their hands. Lana and Neil dutifully followed her.

Next, they went to a safari park. Lana was very calm, but Freeda was overjoyed. She found the moment a monkey excreted onto the side mirror of the car extremely funny and managed to take about a dozen photos of the pissing monkey.

They visited the Harry Potter Museum, Madame Tussauds, the London Eye… They also dropped in at the National Gallery and quickly turned around, as it obviously could not compete with other places on the entertainment program - like Leicester Square with the world's largest M&M store. Freeda was overwhelmed by this huge chocolate world! She ran from floor to floor, her eyes beaming with happiness, and the adults could hardly keep up. They came out of the store exhausted, with large bags filled with chocolate and a bunch of other M&M memorabilia.

The culinary choices impressed Freeda most of all: Italian, Greek, Chinese and Indian cuisine, English pubs, and small coffee shops. Freeda ate nonstop, almost like she had never been fed in her life, and Neil was happy to accommodate any and all of her gastronomic desires.

They were also lucky with the weather, the days being warm and sunny. Freeda was astonished.

'How can it be that it does not rain in London?'

Then, as if by magic, it began to drizzle. The rain ended very quickly, but Freeda was happy and even tried to capture this event with her camera.

Lana and Neil only had nights at their disposal; wonderful nights, full of love, passion, and tenderness...

***

At the airport, Neil cried. Freeda could hardly hold back her tears, too.

'He will come to us now, won't he?' she asked, pleadingly after parting with Neil.

'Of course! He will come in August,' Lana replied.

Freeda was very pleased with the answer but did not show any emotion.

When the plane took off, Lana looked down at the small island with fond feeling, watching it slowly shrink into the distance, trying to feel if she could live in this place.

Her heart replied, confidently: *Yes, I can!*

Chapter 25: Boy

On a hot August day, Lana and Freeda met Neil at Odessa Airport. They easy recognised him in the crowd at arrivals; he stood out! Bright red trousers, yellow polo, blue baseball cap... It was obvious that he had made an effort to look (he thought) fashionable.

'You look so... colourful,' Lana said, smiling and kissing him.

'I thought you'd appreciate my style,' he replied with a laugh.

On that same day, Freeda dragged everyone to the shopping centre to completely change Neil's apparel, where she chose fashionable jeans, two pairs of shoes and several expensive shirts. Neil was very pleased with his new image, and Freeda appointed herself as his personal stylist. (For many years following, Neil was not allowed to buy anything for himself without her prior approval.)

Lana was never a big fan of cooking. Fortunately, she did not have to cook, since her mother lived nearby and happily cooked for her beloved girls. But, Lana wanted to cook something special for Neil, herself. Fish, pilaf, vegetable salads and apple pie, she did her best to impress Neil with her cooking. Later, she found out that Neil did not like hardly any of it, but he heroically ate everything, including borscht and soups cooked by Lana's mother.

Gradually, all the dishes disappeared from their regular menu, but Lana tormented Neil with "masterpieces" of culinary art for several more years.

***

They lived from meeting to meeting: Neil visited them, they flew to him, or they all travelled somewhere together. Neil tried always to organise the joint trips to be interesting to Freeda, like a trip to Disneyland Paris. So that the girl would not be bored, Neil offered to take "The Boy" with them — the nickname of Lana's nephew, the son of her sister, Tina.

In Paris, Lana decided to combine entertainment for children with a cultural program and dragged them all out to the Louvre on the very first day. It was not crowded and, surprisingly, there was no queue.

Perhaps, there is no queue because it is Monday, Lana thought. 'How lucky we are!' she exclaimed with delight.

Imagine her disappointment when they found that the Louvre was closed on Mondays.

'Hurray!' the children shouted, jumping for joy, and clapping their hands ("children" being two children and one adult man).

'Well, we'll come here another day. Let's go to the Orsay Museum instead!' Lana upset the "children".

While Lana passed from hall to hall, enjoying the paintings of her favourite impressionists, the "children" examined all the benches and seating places in the museum, every one they passed. After that, to somehow compensate for the "wasted time", Neil suggested that they go somewhere for dinner. Everyone gladly agreed.

For the next few days, they ventured into the magical world of Disneyland. Fearless Freeda wanted to try all the slides and rides. They hoped very much that the Boy would keep her company in most of them, freeing adults from the duty and giving them the opportunity to stay chatting for a little while.

One attraction which everyone went on was the Hollywood Tower Hotel. It seemed very scary, and the Boy never even opened his eyes, so they had to tell him what was inside. After hearing about it, he wanted to go inside.

But, standing in a huge queue at one of the most popular rides was too much. When there were only a few people left in front of them, the Boy unexpectedly jumped out of the queue, sat down on a bench, and announced that he had changed his mind and did not want to go on it.

'You are afraid!' Freeda teased.

'I'm not afraid,' the Boy said, voice trembling. 'I just don't want to go there.'

Neil sat down next to him and said, 'To be honest, I don't want to go there either, because I'm afraid.'

'You see, Neil is scared, too!' the Boy shouted to Freeda, betraying his true reason for the change of mind.

As a result, Lana had to keep her daughter company on the ride. She thought her brain, eyes, and heart would fall out; it was so scary. She prayed nonstop and crossed herself with relief when the nightmare was over.

The rest of the visit included photographs with Mickey Mouse, various souvenirs assimilated, almost all catering establishments visited, and one evening they enjoyed a fabulous fireworks display over the Sleeping Beauty Castle.

* * *

They also visited the Louvre, and walked around Paris for a long time, took pictures near the Eiffel Tower and ate very tasty crepes with chocolate and banana. Even the very cold weather could not spoil the trip – everyone was pleased and happy. The children were having fun and just playing around.

Then the party entered the Metro. There were two escalators moving up in parallel. Continuing to play around, the children decided to race each other to the top. The Boy jumped on one moving staircase and the others stepped on the other one.

The Boy's escalator was always slightly ahead of the other. Seeing the end of her staircase, the girl was about to make the final dash to get ahead of the Boy, when they realised, they had already arrived, and the other escalator was continuing up to another level. Suddenly anticipated joy of winning was instantly replaced with terror. In search of the child, they ran chaotically through the huge metro station from one end to the other.

'Follow me!' Lily cried, appearing from nowhere.

Freeda suddenly changed direction and ran the opposite way. Lana and Neil rushed after her. A moment later they saw the Boy, surrounded by a crowd of people speaking to him in French.

'Mum! Mum!' the crowd shouted joyfully when saw Lana running up with goggled eyes and began to applaud.

Crying, she hugged, kissed, and praised the child for his courage. He was a hero that evening because he was not scared, did not run around the station in search of his stupid "parents", but simply stood at the end of the staircase and waited patiently, protected by some disapproving French adults.

***

In a busy cafe at Paris Charles de Gaulle Airport, the children finished their breakfast, while Lana and Neil drank coffee.

Two policemen approached the tables one after the other, and people immediately began to leave the cafe.

'French? English?' asked the policemen coming up to their company.

'English,' Neil replied.

Without saying anything, the guardians continued their round. More people got up and left.

Suddenly, someone came up to their table and explained in English: "Evacuation".

It turned out that someone had left a bag near the cafe, so it was decided to evacuate this part of the airport in case it contained a bomb.

'They only care about the Frenchmen, and don't care about the Englishers,' Neil said.

The joke defused the tension, but the company hurriedly left the cafe, leaving their half-eaten breakfast.

The rest of the time they spent in the waiting area. At some point, the Boy approached Neil and sat down next to him. Without saying anything, he hugged Neil's shoulder and pressed against him tightly, as if trying to show his love and respect.

Chapter 26: Snowstorm, or Meeting the Parents

A month after returning from Paris, the girls were going on a new journey, this time to Neil's homeland.

The plan was to depart from Kiev to London but, the day before their departure, the weather in Kiev changed for the worse. At first it was just snowing, then a severe blizzard began. Lana continually checked the departure information as flights were cancelled one by one.

***

'I already can feel this trip will be hard work,' Nicky muttered irritably.

'We will manage, Nicky!' Lily answered with enthusiasm. *'We've dealt with more difficult situations!'*

***

Not wanting to accept that the trip would be cancelled, Lana checked the airport website and the weather forecast continuously. Unfortunately, everything indicated that the weather would get even worse the next day.

Suddenly Lana's travel agent called and advised to get to the airport as early as possible and be one of the first in the airline's office.

'It is their responsibility to get you to London. You might be lucky,' she said.

They raced to the airport and were second in line in the airline's office. Though it seemed an eternity until the first passenger left the office, Lana noticed they were smiling as they left.

A quarter of an hour later, Lana and Freeda sent Neil a photo of their new tickets; travelling on the same day but diverted via Vienna.

***

'We did it!' Lily exclaimed, but Nicky did not share her optimism.
'This is just the beginning…'

***

Despite the bad weather sweeping rapidly through the whole of Europe, Lana and Freeda flew to London with little disruption. Neil met them at the airport and, tired but happy, they set off towards a cottage that Neil had rented especially for this visit, in a picturesque place north of London.

It was snowing in England, too, which amused them very much at first.

'No matter how far we ran, the blizzard caught up with us!' Lana said, laughing.

But the snow quickly became stronger and stronger, and a real blizzard began, making driving difficult.

Neil's sat-nav took them to the cottage by the shortest route, sometimes through country roads and fields. When they were less than fifteen minutes from the cottage, their car suddenly got stuck in the snow on one of these quiet country lanes in the middle of a field. There were no other cars in sight.

They tried to push the car out, but this only made the situation worse. The car was at an angle, blocking the road and stuck with its rear wheel in a small ditch separating the field from the road. They decided to walk out, onto the highway, and try to find some help.

It snowed incessantly. It was dark and very cold. They put on more warm clothes, took a small bag with the essentials, and wandered toward the most recent main road.

To Freeda, this whole situation seemed very funny. She laughed and took a lot of pictures.

'Aren't you scared?' Lana asked.

'Not at all,' her daughter replied lightly. 'I'm sure Neil will think of something!'

Lana looked at Neil.

He does look pretty confident.

They spent about an hour on the main road, but only a few cars passed, and none of them stopped. Neil tried to call a taxi, but this was also impossible, since there was no phone connection in these backwoods.

There was a single house not far from the road. They knocked on the door. Nobody opened it.

***

'What now? They've tried everything,' Nicky said.

'Yes, now it's our turn!' Lily exclaimed, rubbing her hands impatiently.

***

Lana suddenly saw the headlights on the other side of the highway, down where they had left their car. It was a car, moving slowly.

'Look! Look!' she shouted, pointing in the direction of the approaching light. 'They will reach our car and have to stop, as it's impossible to pass it. Let's run, quickly! Between us we'll find a solution.'

Feet sinking in the snow, they ran back towards the country road, their eyes fixed on the headlights slowly approaching. But the car managed to pass the section of the road they had blocked without any problems, and began to approach the highway, speeding up.

'Faster! Faster!' Lana urged everyone, worried to miss the last hope of salvation.

They ran to the road, crossing at the same time as the approaching car and, waving their hands, stopped it. It was a large off-road vehicle with a young male driver and woman passenger. The strangers immediately guessed that they were stopped by the owners of the car left in the middle of the field.

'Just a mile from here, we have a cottage that we are renting out. It is empty today. You can spend the night there, and you can deal with your car and leave tomorrow morning,' they suggested.

The unfortunate travellers agreed without hesitation, especially as they had no other option. Neil climbed into the boot as Lana and Freeda got into the back seat, where they found a toddler with blond curly hair sitting between them in a child seat.

'Don't you think he looked like an angel?' Lana asked Freeda quietly, getting out of the car. Freeda agreed.

The owners of the cottage showed them where to leave the key when they left the next day and asked them not to worry about payment – despite Neil's insistence to let him thank them for their help. (Neil later won this argument.) They apologised for not having any food with them, but said there was coffee, tea, and sugar in the kitchen.

    The cottage turned out to be extremely nice and cosy. On the ground floor there was a small living room, with a fireplace and TV set, as well as a small kitchenette.

    Freeda began to survey the house, starting from the kitchen and putting the kettle on. At that moment, someone knocked on the door. It was the hostess of the cottage. Apologizing once again for the lack of food, she offered a cup of milk. It was so nice of her!

    They sat by the fireplace for a long time, enjoyed coffee with milk, and cookies unexpectedly found in the bag, and chatted about the incredible story of their salvation. After taking hot showers, everyone went to their bedrooms: Freeda on the second floor, Lana and Neil in the bedroom in the attic.

***

    Early the next morning, Neil quietly rose and went to rescue the car. Lana looked out the window to see a beautiful bright sunny day. Everything was covered with fresh snow, sparkling, white and beautiful. She called to Freeda and the girls basked in the bed for two hours, enjoying the crisp snow-white bedding until Neil returned and told them his amazing story.

From afar, he had seen a line of cars parked on both sides of his car. It was obvious that the road was blocked and impossible to drive by. He was mentally preparing to listen to the curses and indignation of all these people. But, as he approached, a tractor appeared and took just a moment to pull out his car, unblocking the road.

'While some were asleep,' Nicky muttered, shaking his head towards Lana and Freeda. *'Some of us were working!'*

'If someone told me such a story, I would never have believed it!' Neil said, ending his story.

I would have believed! Lana noticed miracles in everything and rejoiced in them like a child.

They packed up, left the keys as agreed, and drove to their cottage.

***

The main purpose of this visit was supposed to be an introduction to Neil's parents. It was decided to meet at a hotel restaurant, where the parents had booked a room specially for this occasion.

'How should we dress?' Lana asked Neil the night before (she had brought a few smart outfits with her, of course).

'Oh, my parents are very relaxed,' Neil replied. 'Jeans and a sweater will be fine.'

Lana put on jeans and chose a top that could be considered both casual and smart… just in case.

They arrived at the hotel at the same time as Neil's parents. When they got out of the car, Neil could not believe his eyes: his dad was wearing a suit, and his mum was wearing a long, elegant coat.

'I have never seen my parents dress like this!' he said with a laugh, while Lana mentally praised herself for her choice of outfit.

'How should we address your parents?' she asked quickly. 'Mr? Mrs?'

'Oh, no! Just Brian and Sheila,' Neil replied.

Neil's parents turned out to be very easy-going people, with dinner being followed by casual conversation. Brian tried to speak loudly and slowly to make it easier for Lana and Freeda to understand him. It was more difficult to understand Sheila but, in general, Lana managed to grasp the meaning of most of what was said. At the end of the dinner, Lana presented them with a table clock with images of one of her favourite paintings by Claude Monet.

***

Later, Lana learned that Neil's parents were shocked when he told them about a serious relationship with a woman from another country and, moreover, that they had met on a dating site. They had thought he would be able to come to terms with his ex-wife and, in time, reconcile.

This desire for his son to return to his marriage was never shown to Lana, in any way. Lana and Freeda always felt truly welcome in their home. Brian and Sheila sincerely rejoiced in Freeda's academic successes, and helped Neil's new family whenever they could.

When Neil adopted Freeda, Sheila cleared her diary and came to celebrate this important event. On the way to the restaurant, she asked Lana, 'Freeda is Neil's daughter now, but who is she for me?'

'It's up to you,' Lana replied.

In a few years, Neil's parents would pass away; first Brian, then Sheila. All five of her grandchildren would be mentioned in her obituary and eulogy: Nicola and Alex (children of Neil's sister), Charlotte and David (children of his brother), and Freeda, Neil's daughter. It turned out that three of the five, Alex, David, and Freeda, were born in the same year.

Chapter 27: Nelson Mandela

The relationship between Lana and Neil was developing rapidly and they were making firm plans for the future, when during a routine medical examination, Lana was given some bad news. The original diagnosis worsened after an additional consultation, and it was recommended that Lana have an operation as soon as possible.

This cannot happen to me! No, no, this is some kind of mistake! Lana couldn't believe what she was going through.

***

'How can we have let her down when she believes in us so much?' Lily asked Nicky.

'Have we ever let her down?' Nicky asked in return.

***

Lana lacked confidence in the recommended solution and decided to check the diagnosis in another country. Her choice was Israel – decisive factors with this destination being she did not need to obtain an entry visa and there was a direct flight from Odessa.

Neil was ready to fly with her, but it was decided that Lana would go there with her mother, and Freeda would stay with Lana's sister Tina for several days.

***

They were met at Tel Aviv Airport by a Russian-speaking agent and taken to a specially rented apartment, not far from the hospital. The first examination was scheduled for the next day.

Lana slept like a baby that night, dreaming about her happy future with Neil. Her mum did not sleep, that night or the following nights. Worried about her daughter's health, she lost so much weight on the short trip that, upon returning home, all her clothes no longer fit her.

Fortunately, the worst diagnosis was not confirmed, but an operation could not be avoided. The doctor promised to send the final diagnosis and costs for the operation in a few days.

Despite the unhappy purpose of the visit, Lana and her mum decided to organise a cultural program for themselves, so as to relax and divert their attention.

They walked along Tel Aviv quay, breathing in the warm Mediterranean air, and even found a favourite restaurant. They went on a city tour and, of course, visited Tel Aviv Museum of Art.

It turned out that this gallery had a relatively large collection, from which Lana wanted to see Kandinsky's and Klimt's paintings the most. Due to the enormous size of the museum, it was not easy to find paintings which interested Lana. They wandered the halls for a long time, until they finally came across a Russian-speaking attendant, who knew absolutely everything about the museum collection and was happy to assist visitors.

'Could you tell us, please, in which room can we find Klimt's painting?' Lana asked.

'But, here it is!' she replied, pointing over Lana's shoulder. 'Right behind you!'

Turning, they saw what they had been looking for – a huge portrait of Friederike Maria Beer.

The attendant explained how to find the Kandinsky's painting and advised on other works worth seeing. They found the room quickly and walked it twice, each time passing a chair on which the museum attendant was sitting but could not find the painting. Then they decided to ask for help.

'Kandinsky, Kandinsky,' they repeated the artist's name several times since this museum attendant did not speak Russian.

'Information, information…' she replied, pointing her hand in the direction of the exit from the hall, making it clear they should go to the information desk and ask there.

Thanking her for her help, Lana and her mother looked up and saw… Kandinsky's work. The painting they couldn't find was right behind the museum attendant's chair!

Barely holding back their laughter, the women left the hall.

***

The day after returning home, Lana received an email with the final (not frightening!) diagnosis and the cost of the operation, which was around the cost of a standard apartment in Odessa! Lana could barely afford such an expensive operation, but she was ready to do it, because she wanted to leave this experience behind as soon as possible.

Her mum supported her, but Neil insisted that the operation be performed in England, saying it would be much cheaper, and he would be there and could look after her. But Lana did not want to have to go through the complex visa issuance procedure and just waste time when it was refused.

***

'How do we convince this silly woman?' Nicky *asked, losing hope.*

'Let's use the heavy artillery!' Lily replied cheerfully.

***

Then, in a sudden change of mind, Lana's mother also began to believe that the operation could best be performed in England. Her arguments succeeded in convincing Lana.

Surprisingly, a visa to England was issued very quickly. And, upon learning about the unhappy purpose of the trip, Lana's manager paid her a one-time bonus which covered all her forthcoming expenses.

***

The operation went smoothly, but Lana felt unbearable pain on regaining consciousness. Fortunately, the nurse immediately noticed and put a control in her hand.

'Press the button every time the pain becomes too much,' she said. Then Lana was taken to a ward.

Neil was shocked at seeing her. He thought it would take her a very long time to recover.

However, Lana began to move about the very next day and even took a shower and changed her clothes without help. The nurses were amazed at her strength.

Undoubtedly, Lana stood out from other patients!

Her ward was more like a hotel room. It had a bathroom, a very comfortable adjustable bed, and a TV set. In the morning she was brought a menu from which she could choose breakfast, lunch, and dinner. Lana sent photos of each menu to Freeda, who gladly helped her mother choose.

Lana did not know how to use the remote control, so she could not change the TV channels and was stuck on news all day long – the main subject of which was the death of Nelson Mandela, former leader of South Africa. She was not bored, though, because Neil spent all his free time with her.

On the day Lana was expected to be discharged, Arsenal had an away football match in Manchester. Neil, who had never missed a single match with his favourite team, tried to persuade Lana that he was ready to miss this one.

***

'How can he not go to such an important match?' Nicky was indignant.

'Can't she ask to be discharged a day later? What's she missing by staying an extra day? She can watch rolling TV news about Nelson Mandela and the food is good!'

***

During doctors' rounds the day before her planned discharge, Lana asked to stay in the hospital for one more night. The doctor was surprised, but did not object, and she persuaded Neil to go to Manchester.

Neil came to the hospital immediately on his return. He was wearing a black jacket with unfamiliar bright yellow spots on it.

'What is it?' Lana asked.

'Probably eggs,' Neil replied, looking at the spots. 'I ate a roll with a sausage and an egg.'

For some reason, this set Lana laughing. She choked with laughter, wiping the remnants of dinner off Neil's jacket, feeling the pain in the stiches not yet healed.

When Neil left, she tried her best not to remember the eggs, as it caused her to laugh and have more pain. She breathed in and out deeply to calm herself, tried to switch over to sad news about Nelson Mandela, but the thought of egg stains on Neil's jacket stubbornly continued to amuse her.

***

Neil looked after her for the next two weeks. He rented a bungalow so that

Lana did not need to climb stairs. He did the obligatory daily physical exercises with her, which Lana found entertaining.

Neil also decided to use this time to acquaint her with his business. She pretended to be trying to keep everything in her mind. Smiling, she looked at Neil with love – *I'll figure it out when the time comes* – and got lost in her dreams!

***

After a scheduled visit to the doctor, she was allowed to return to Odessa, and Neil arrived two weeks later to celebrate the New Year together.

At the New Year party, he unexpectedly knelt, handed Lana a beautiful velvet box containing a diamond ring and began to talk very quickly.

Lana did not understand a word, but smiled, kissed him, took the coveted ring, and said, 'Yes, I do!'

Chapter 28: Not Your Country

They decided not to delay the wedding, but a check of the website of Arsenal football club (an essential requirement!) showed that the nearest free date was mid-March. It was a good date, even symbolic, falling exactly two years from the moment of their first meeting.

Lana took the preparations for the wedding very seriously: an expensive restaurant overlooking the sea was found and booked, a menu chosen, photographer and cars found, and invitations to close friends and relatives sent. The bride considered every smallest detail of her appearance for the day – dress, hairstyle, jewellery, bridal bouquet – everything had to look harmonious and elegant.

Neil was entrusted to buy a suit on his own but, just in case, he bought a couple and sent photos to Freeda for approval. She disapproved of both but chose the least worst in order to avoid tormenting the groom. That suit was also the closest match to the bride's dress.

***

'We will have our wedding in March and apply immediately for immigration visas. Freeda's school year ends in May and, if everything goes well, we will move to England in the summer. She will go to high school there in September.'

Lana was sharing her plans with friend, Victoria, over dinner in a Japanese restaurant.

Victoria was Lana's former student. They became close friends because she had a similar situation — following Lana's advice, she met a man from Germany on a dating site. Their marriage was due to take place in April, just a month after the wedding of Lana and Neil. They recalled how they met, how they became friends, how they met their men, discussed their prospective new lives and were very happy for each other.

'The only thing I'll miss,' Lana said with a laugh, 'is my mink coat. There are strong views against wearing natural fur, so in England I will have to buy a fake fur coat.'

'And me, too,' agreed Victoria, laughing. 'When Jörg saw my fur coat, he said that this is no longer "fashionable" in Germany.'

At that moment a message from Freeda arrived.

'What are you eating?' Lana took a photo of her sushi and sent it.

'Lucky you… I'm sitting here hungry.' Freeda's reply was accompanied by sad emojis.

***

'Babushka, why don't you feed the girl?' Lana asked, laughing, when she returned home.

Lana's mother was renamed "Babushka" (the Russian word for Granny) some time ago. It was also easy for Neil to call her that, since he knew the word from the song belted out by his favourite singer, Kate Bush.

'What is she saying?' Babushka was indignant. 'The fridge is full of saucepans!'

'Exactly! Only saucepans!' Freeda noted, demonstratively opening the fridge door.

***

From Neil's side, his friend Derek with wife Angela, and Brian and Sheila, were coming to the wedding. Everyone was due to arrive on the same day, but Sheila forgot her passport and they had to rebook their flight for the next day.

Neil could not contain his delight when he saw Lana on the day of the wedding: her hair elegantly put up instead of its usual loose style, stunning dress, earrings matching her hair, natural makeup… 'You are so beautiful!' he said.

When Lana saw Neil in his new suit, the overly cropped trousers immediately caught her eye.

'I'll let them out quickly, now,' Babushka volunteered to help.

'It's okay, these are minor things! I will try not to look at them,' Lana said, laughing.

The couple had agreed that, at the wedding ceremony, Lana would pronounce the marriage vows in English and Neil in Russian. Lana learned her speech by heart and spoke it well, with expression and tone. Neil tried to memorize his words, but at the ceremony decided just to repeat the vow after the registrar.

(It should be noted that Neil decided to study Russian and bought an expensive audio training program for this purpose, which he listened to in the car during long drives to football matches, tormenting Derek asleep next to him. "My favourite toy is a tractor. The mining industry. I work in the fashion industry," … a female voice spoke from the disc, pronouncing each word clearly and slowly. Lana commented that the female voice had strange grammar and syntax, but Neil stubbornly continued to learn all these useless sentences and phrases.)

After the wedding ceremony, everyone went to a restaurant, where the tables were overflowing with food. There was so much that, in his toast, Brian joked, "I noticed that you all eat a lot."

Lana's sister Tina toasted in return: "We not only eat a lot, we also drink a lot!"

It was fun, and somehow everyone understood each other.

The next day, the company split into two groups: the men went to the local brewery to watch the Arsenal vs. Tottenham football match, the women went to the Opera House for a ballet. Both parties reunited for a dinner at a restaurant near the Londonskaya hotel, where the English guests were staying.

The weather was wonderful, very warm, and sunny. They walked along Deribasovskaya Street and Primorsky Boulevard and enjoyed delicious food in a local restaurant. Everyone was delighted with the city! Beautiful Odessa showed its true colours to its visitors from England.

Later, Sheila remembered that many years ago, during a cruise on the Black Sea, she had already visited Odessa and even found postcards with the image of the famous Odessa Opera House bought during that trip.

***

Lana only announced the marriage to her colleagues after the wedding.

'I have two pieces of news for you,' she began. 'First, I got married!'

Everyone began to congratulate her, and the room got louder.

'Second, I married an Englishman!'

The room got quieter.

'So, you will leave us? When?'

'It will depend on how quickly we obtain visas. The procedure can take a long time,' Lana replied, calming her colleagues a little.

But they obtained visas very quickly. (Perhaps the officer examining their documents fell to the pressure of reams of tender correspondence and dozens of photographs with which Lana supported her case.)

By this time, Freeda had graduated with honours from her school, and Neil found a high school in England for her. For enrolment, it was necessary to provide a document with grades and have an interview via Skype. During the interview, Freeda answered all the questions only 'Yes' or 'No', nevertheless she was admitted and enrolled for the new school year in September.

It was also time to part with Marisa, Lana's beloved car. A month before leaving, Lana posted an ad on the Internet, which was immediately answered by several people, but Lana decided to sell the car only to a person she liked. She really wanted Marisa to fall into good hands. Such a buyer was found. He was ready to pick up the car immediately, but Lana told him that she would sell the car in a month, and he agreed.

The buyer called on the agreed day and said that the price of cars had dropped in a last month. Lana knew this but said that her car was worth the same as a month ago. He did not argue and paid the amount agreed at the start. Lana was very sad to part with Marisa, but she was reassured by the fact that she would be well cared for in her new owner's hands.

At work, the team said goodbye to her generously.

They had dinner at a luxurious restaurant with their friends.

Flight tickets were bought, and bags packed.

Thus, everything was ready for their departure.

***

The day before leaving, Neil and Lana walked for a long time along the sea, starting from the Golden Coast beach and reaching the 10th Station of the Big Fountain. Lana was enjoying beautiful views of the sea sparkling in the sun and eagerly inhaled the warm sea air.

'I guess you will miss this very much, living in England,' Neil said, noticing with sadness how his wife looked at the sea she had adored since childhood, which had become an integral part of her life.

Only now did Lana suddenly feel some fear, starkly realising that she would start a completely new life in another country in just one day from now. It also dawned on her that, now she would be fully responsible for Freeda – in practice, until now, her daughter was actually raised by Babushka.

Who's going to cook? Her mother had always been the family cook. *My English in not good enough…*

The more she thought, the more anxious she became.

Divining her concern, Neil tried to reassure his wife. 'Don't worry, all will be well.'

An interesting episode from her past sprang to mind in that moment.

Shortly before meeting Freeda's father, her best friend, (who had introduced them) had dragged Lana to a fortune teller. 'You will see, what she says will come true,' her friend assured her.

Lana expected to see an old woman who resembled a witch. The fortune teller turned out to be an ordinary middle-aged woman who, while cooking something in the kitchen, glanced at Lana's hand and said: 'Oh, this is not your country! You will live somewhere else.' Lana did not attach any importance to these words at the time, but now...

Maybe she could really see that?

This memory, as well as the support of her husband and mother, gave her strength. Lana dismissed all fears and doubts and looked forward to the future with hope.

She had huge plans for the future, the most important of which was to be happy!

***

'Don't worry, we are always there for you!' Lily encouraged her.

'I'll take a couple of weeks off to get some rest,' Nicky said. 'We have a lot more to do...'

Part IV - Happiness

Chapter 29: His World

In England, they settled in a small town in Essex, where they rented a house not far from Freeda's school. Lana immediately set about turning it into a home. All the rooms were furnished within a month, and Neil was amazed at how a rented property could so quickly have the feeling of a personal space.

Lana felt comfortable and relaxed in her new home, but any contact with the outside world was highly stressful, thanks to the language barrier. She worried people might not understand her, or she might make an inappropriate reply and would look stupid. Indeed, she did not understand much at first and gave incorrect responses, but she continued to force herself to leave the comfort of their home.

In a local store worked a young guy with special needs. One day he showed friendship towards Lana, then, every time she came, he began to talk to her.

'He just wants to help,' a shop assistant explained in his defence. Lana accepted his help, kindly given, and always tried to say something pleasant in response.

She also found she had to regularly cook for the first time in her life. She undertook this responsibility herself, following the traditions of her family – serving soups and other basic dishes that no one liked. Later, she would share this domestic duty with Neil and Freeda, and Sunday Roast, Italian pasta, and other dishes more enjoyed by British families gradually replaced Lana's more traditional menu, to the household's great relief.

***

It was also decided that Lana would help in her husband's business.

She started with criticism. In her opinion, nothing was well organised, starting with the allocation of work and especially with the accounting software. Lana naturally continued to behave like the chief accountant of a large international company, while Neil waited patiently for her to grasp reality and accept his business was a simpler venture. Eventually, Lana realised that her continuing criticism only interfered with work. Then they divided responsibilities, and it quickly became easier for everyone.

In the beginning, Lana went to the office every day, then started to work from home to help Freeda with her studies. She was very happy with this arrangement. First, there was no need to spend two hours commuting. Second, she could pick up Freeda from school each day. Best of all, there was no need to communicate in English with customers and employees!

One morning, though, Neil called unexpectedly and asked Lana to come to the office. He had to leave for a couple of hours for a meeting in another town, and he was the only one in the office that day. Hearing this was a real shock: she must drive herself there, then answer phone calls and communicate with customers for two hours, and then complete the challenging drive home. Such horrible experiences!

Neil did not insist, he was ready to just close the office, but that would be not best for the business – so he asked Lana to help.

No, I cannot! was the first thought that flashed through her head, but somehow, her mouth replied, 'I'll come right now,' and she began to get ready.

But Lana was fretting while getting ready. *How will I drive there on my own? I have never driven there myself; Neil always drives!*

'It's a piece of cake!' Nicky replied. 'Just turn on the sat-nav and go!'

Lana got behind the wheel, turned on the sat-nav, crossed herself and drove off. The road was very easy, and she was there in less than an hour.

The next challenge was paying for parking. Lana had never really figured out how to use the parking meter, since Neil always did it.

'Everything is clearly written there, just read it carefully,' Nicky offered his helpful advice once again.

The instructions on the parking meter turned out to be simple and understandable, and she quickly did everything required.

Walking up to the office, Lana felt heroic! Neil was waiting for her at the entrance.

'You don't have to answer the phone calls if you don't want to. I'll be back in a couple of hours,' he said, leaving quickly.

Lana stared at the phone in horror. *Maybe I'll be lucky, and no one will call at all.*

As if hearing this, the phone rang. Lana froze. Then her hand went towards the phone, but she hesitated.

'Don't be afraid, pick up the phone!' Lily encouraged.

Lana grabbed the receiver. It was one of the landlords, asking for a copy of an old contract. Lana had recently drawn up documents for this landlord to organise the return of a deposit, so she was aware of his situation. She easily found the right contract and sent it on.

Encouraged by this first success, Lana decided to answer all the phone calls! There were quite a lot of them. She conscientiously noted every detail so Neil could call back those customers that Lana could not help.

At least there are no visitors, she thought, answering another call. In the very next moment, the office door opened, and an elderly lady entered. Smiling, Lana greeted her, and tried to cover her fear.

'Just smile, listen, and agree with everything she says. Nothing else is required of you!' Lily gave some quick instructions.

The woman turned out to be a neighbour of one of the tenants. She did not need anything; she just came in to complain. Lana found out later that she did it regularly just because she was bored. After speaking out, she left the office, pleased that she had been heard.

The next to visit the office was a young woman with a child in a pushchair. She had come to collect her mail from her previous property. Lana did not know anything about this and asked her to come the next day when there would be employees in the office who could help. But, the

123

woman categorically stated that she was not going to come tomorrow, that she needed her mail today. Now.

'Her letters are in the most obvious place! Can't you see them?' Lily was circling over the stack of envelopes lying on the table next to the printer.

Lana looked desperately around the office, and then she noticed something that looked like mail on a small table. She checked the name; this was it! Smiling, the woman thanked Lana for her assistance and, taking her letters and pushchair, left the office.

Neil returned four hours later due to a traffic jam, and Lana was very happy to see him! She suddenly felt terribly tired, but she was incredibly proud of herself – although she would not want to repeat such a feat again.

* * *

Lana did not find driving in England easy.

'Why are you afraid?' Neil wondered. 'You were such a confident driver in Odessa, where you need to have three pairs of eyes in order to simultaneously avoid stray animals crossing the streets, drivers who don't follow any traffic rules, and dodge potholes.'

But, Lana was afraid and did not even try to deny it!

First, it was difficult for her to get used to driving on the "wrong" side of the road. 'Left, left, left,' she would remind herself each time taking the wheel. But sometimes she automatically swerved to the right anyway.

Secondly, narrow roads and fast-moving traffic frightened her. The route to school had this challenge every day. Seeing approaching cars, Lana's heart began to pound, and when a double-decker school bus appeared in the oncoming lane, she simply stopped and let it drive by. The bus driver thanked her every time, not realizing that Lana was doing this out of sheer fear, not politeness.

It was necessary to obtain a UK driving license within a year of arriving to England. Lana first passed the theory exam, getting almost the maximum marks, but there were big doubts that she would be able to pass the driving test on the first try. Lana hired an instructor and learnt all the local roads in just four lessons, then went to sit the test.

After completing the exam, Neil and Freeda came up to her, ready to utter words of support and sympathy – but Lana sang 'La-la-la!' and waved her passing certificate!

But having passed the exam did not make her a confident driver. She still forced herself to take the wheel, every time.

***

However, all these problems were minor in comparison with football, which took up a huge part of her husband's life. Lana was not prepared for his "hobby" to absorb so much of his time, and she showed her displeasure in every possible way.

"I presume you want Arsenal to lose," Neil noted once. Lana was very surprised – she was engrossed in the thought of her daughter's studies, not in football.

Once, having lost his season ticket, Neil decided that Lana had thrown it away. Although the ticket was found on the same day and Neil apologized immediately, Lana realised that somewhere she had crossed the line, and her husband saw her as a threat to his hobby. Her constant dissatisfaction was clearly not helpful for their relationship. And although they had never had quarrels, Lana still did not feel truly happy.

***

'I think we need to intervene here,' Nicky noticed. 'I'm even ready to deal with it personally. Football is serious cause!'

He dropped some lines on Lana's Facebook profile.

***

Lana unexpectedly received a message from her friend, who had evolved from being a successful financial manager to a relationship expert. 'When you have time, listen to my webinar. I would like to know your opinion.' Out of respect for her friend, Lana decided to listen to it.

'When you choose a man, you accept his world. Take a close look at what surrounds him. Is it right for you? Do you like it? Because having chosen this man, you should accept his world...'

Lana stopped the recording and listened to this passage again: "When you choose a man, you choose his world, too..."

Suddenly, she felt an influx of immense happiness.

Of course, how simple it is! I always knew that he loved football. He has never hidden it! Everything suited me. And what has changed now? Nothing!

Lana felt relieved when she realised this. She did not need to fight; she just needed to accept the world of the man she loved so much.

From that moment on, the football became a source of joy for her. Now they travelled together more often, and while Neil watched the game, Lana and Freeda surveyed local places of interest or just went shopping, and then the family dined at a local restaurant.

Thanks to football, they visited Victoria and Jörg in Germany, as well as Barcelona, Paris, Monaco, Nice and many other beautiful places.

"Life is good!" Neil would repeat often, and Lana absolutely agreed with him.

Chapter 30: Bublik and Bulochka

When Freeda was six years old, long before they moved to England, Lana gave her a toy rabbit. She just could not resist buying it when she saw it sitting alone on the shelf of a toy shop, looking at her with his sad, beady, black eyes.

'What a cutie!' Freeda said picking up her new toy. 'What is his name?'

'Bublik!' Babushka answered confidently. 'His name is Bublik!' (Which means bagel in Russian.)

Freeda and Lana looked closely at the rabbit and agreed that there was simply no better name for him.

So, they had a new and very important family member — a cuddly toy rabbit named Bublik.

To be honest, Freeda wasn't particularly interested in him, since he turned out to be a big bore. One of his favourite activities was to have educational conversations with her in a voice reminiscent of her mother. For instance, Freeda did not like to read, but Bublik told her a lot about the benefits of reading.

In contrast, a toy monkey named Martyha urged the girl in a disgusting squeaky voice to not waste time reading stupid books – and once even promised to reward her with a banana if she did not read a page for the whole day! Though, when Martyha brought a banana and handed it solemnly to Freeda in the evening, she refused to eat it for some reason.

When Neil appeared in Lana's life, Bublik tried his best to remain silent, as he did not want to scare the man ahead of time and ruin Lana's happiness. However, upon arrival in England, he broke free and started speaking immediately, and confidently, in English. Neil was shocked at how they had managed to hide such an important family member from him for such a long time, but he immediately fell in love with Bublik, despite all his tediousness and love of reading books.

Under their first Christmas tree as a family was a gift for Bublik — a white plush bunny, who was named Bulochka (or bun in Russian). Bulochka became a mediator between Lana and Neil. When Lana needed to discuss some not very comfortable topics with her husband, Bulochka got boldly down to business, and Neil, as a rule, could not resist her charms.

While Bulochka was a homebody, Bublik was happy to keep Lana and Neil company on all their travels, often putting them in awkward situations. So, when they ordered a table for three (for themselves and a friend who was supposed to join them later) in the restaurant in Barcelona, the waiter asked pointing to the plush rabbit: 'Who is the third? Him?'

When Freeda was visiting Oxford University for the final school exam preparation courses, it was decided during a family conference (comprising Lana and Bulochka) that Bublik would accompany her.

'You will be there all alone! You need someone dear next to you,' Lana persuaded her daughter.

Not resisting for long, Freeda agreed but… In Oxford, in order not to embarrass herself, she hid Bublik in her bag and took him out only before going to bed, when no one could see him. When Freeda's new friends confessed at a farewell dinner that some of them had also brought toys, teddy bears and foxes, she felt relief and admitted bringing her bunny.

Bublik, on the other hand, returned from Oxford looking very grand and intelligent and, subsequently giving advice to Neil, continuously reminded him that his opinion was worth listening to, since *he was at Oxford*! For some reason, though, Neil trusted Bulochka's advice more.

Friends of Lana and Neil perceived the "talking" rabbit differently.

'Is she serious?' the husband of one of Lana's friends asked in bewilderment after meeting Bublik and Bulochka.

Others accepted them unconditionally.

'You're gorgeous!' another friend said to Bulochka. 'It seems to me you are trying to appear worse than you really are,' she continued, speaking directly to Bublik.

Some of their friends and acquaintances even had their own "Bubliks" and "Bulochkas," especially families with small children (or not very obedient husbands!).

Chapter 31: Emily, or Friends Come Suddenly

'You must do everything to get the best results you can!' Lana beseeched her daughter. 'Your options for further education will depend on this, and so will your future career.'

Freeda knew this and was very determined, but Lana worried. *Will she have enough commitment for three long years?* Freeda would have to study an extra year since English was not her first language.

But her loving parents did not leave their child to struggle with English education alone. The most challenging subjects were divided fairly: Lana got mathematics and Spanish, Neil got economics and English.

At school, mathematics was Lana's favourite subject. She was very lucky to have had good teachers, who gave such deep knowledge that she still retained it. This gave her the confidence that she could easily assist her daughter. The reality turned out to be very different.

The subject Freeda studied was much more complex, with virtually no similarities to Lana's school curriculum. But the purposeful mother was not going to give up. She studied the school textbook, paragraph by paragraph, to help Freeda with her homework. It even seemed to Lana that she understood some topics better than Freeda. Poor Freeda! Her head was filled with a bunch of other subjects, but Lana believed that mathematics was the most important one and insisted it be prioritized. They frequently argued about it, often reverting to speaking in their own language.

'Why in Russian?' Neil asked jokingly at such moments, trying to defuse the situation.

'Because we don't know so many bad words in English,' Lana replied with a laugh.

Sometimes, when she got angry, Lana could use some really strong words. It mainly happened when she scolded her daughter.

Once, when Freeda was about eight years old, Lana scolded her fiercely. As the rant ended, imperious to her mother's mood, Freeda noted, 'You forgot to say "damn" three times!' Lana burst out laughing but, after this, she always tried harder to control herself.

Unlike Maths, home classes in Economics were very relaxed. Sitting on the sofa, Neil and Freeda were just talking, exchanging opinions, or discussing some topics and ideas. That was not the kind of assistance Lana expected from her husband. However, at the first parent meeting the teacher told them that Freeda began to make progress in

Economics, much to Lana's surprise. *He just wants to provide some encouragement*, Lana thought, then. But at the end of the school year, Freeda was the only one in her class to receive an award "for achievements in Economics."

Freeda finished the first school year with such a high result that the school administration decided not to leave her for another year in the same grade after all, but progress immediately to the next grade.

***

At the beginning of the next school year, her final year of secondary school, it was necessary to choose her preferred university. Although Freeda's school achievements were very impressive, the result was not quite high enough to choose a university from the top level, according to Lana.

Freeda had a whole year to further improve her grades, but her mother believed that it was worth playing it safe and choosing a less prestigious institution, because if the necessary grades are not achieved, it can become a lottery. Freeda obstinately disagreed and decided to apply for her chosen subject at an elite English university.

Unable to convince her daughter directly, Lana decided to recruit her husband to join the argument on her behalf. She came to the negotiations fully equipped with thorough knowledge, taking Bulochka with her. Bulochka, with her insinuating voice, got immediately to the point. But Neil confidently resisted Bulochka's pressure.

'Freeda will decide. But, personally, I support her choice. She's a clever girl!'

Lana and Bulochka had to retreat.

Freeda passed all her exams in mid-May, and a nervous period of waiting for results began.

***

The graduation and Prom took place in June. A beautiful long dress was acquired for the ceremony, along with a cocktail dress, into which Freeda was due to change for the Prom. As always, she was late and, in a hurry, forgot to take her cocktail dress.

'So, you will not change into it!' Lana said flatly, riding in the car on the way to the event. She was terribly irritated by her daughter's disorganization, but there was really no time to go back to pick up the dress.

When the parents returned home, Neil found the forgotten dress and drove it to Freeda, making her incredibly happy.

'What a nice guy!' Lily exclaimed. *'I can never stop liking him!'*

***

The exam results were due to be published on the website at 2 p.m. on an appointed day. On that day, Neil left for work as usual, but Lana and Freeda were so anxious they could not concentrate on anything else.

'Well, shall we go to check the results?' the daughter asked her mother a couple of minutes before the appointed time. They rushed to the computer as fast as they could and, a moment later, the house was filled with shouts of joy! The girls jumped up and down, danced and hugged.

Then they saw a car approaching. Neil had been also unable to sit in the office and tried to get home by the time the results were released. Seeing the happy faces of his beloved girls, the outcome was immediately clear.

'Is this REALLY my result?' Freeda asked jokingly, having re-checked the information on the website, just in case. This WAS her result! She got the highest possible marks in Economics, though Maths was her least impressive mark.

The very next day, Freeda received confirmation of her admission to the Business Management Department at Exeter

University, and a couple of days later she received a nice postcard from her grandmother, Sheila: "Well done, Freeda xxx."

***

While Lana was most worried about her daughter's studies all these years, Freeda was worried about something completely different; she had no friends – or rather, it seemed to her that she had no friends.

'How are you?' Lana asked her daughter one day as she returned from school. 'How was Maths?'

'Awful,' she answered. 'I have no friends…'

Freeda repeated this phrase almost every day. Of course, she communicated with classmates but, unfortunately, she could not call any of them her friend.

'I need to buy new pyjamas to look nice in the mornings,' Lana's daughter said one day.

'In case your friends come?' Lana teased.

'Funny…' Freeda responded, sadly.

Lana tried to support her daughter.

'You have no friends because you repeat it so often. You claim that you do not have them, so the Universe does not grant you friends. Try to switch your focus from "I don't have" to "I have" and the Universe will hear you and immediately find you a real friend!'

***

'Is it you who gave her this "bright" idea?' Nicky asked Lily.
'No, she thought of that herself,' Lily replied. *'I will arrange everything, just do not undermine her!'*

***

A gorgeous blonde beauty named Emily appeared in Freeda's life a month later. From a different class, it turned out that Emily had noticed Freeda as soon as she appeared at their school and had decided that she wanted to be her friend. With all her might, she had tried to attract the attention of the newcomer, greeting, and talking when she could. But Freeda was so sure that no one was seriously interested in her friendship that she simply did not notice.

Emily still managed to pierce Freeda's armour, and they went on a school trip to Madrid together.

Emily became not only a real friend of Freeda, but also a very close person to the family. She called Lana "my second mother", and she joined them on various family trips.

***

'Freeda, put on nice pyjamas, what if friends come suddenly?' Lana joked to her daughter the day before her eighteenth birthday. And friends did come! Emily showed up with gifts, cake, and champagne early in the morning. Then they all went to a fancy restaurant in London.

On their return from London, Freeda invited her dad to the pub. She was eager to treat him to a glass of beer, and eager to show her ID card – which confirmed that she was eighteen and could legally buy alcohol. However, to her great disappointment, confirmation of age was not required that first time.

Chapter 32: Just Coincidences

Lana soon realised that the university degrees and accounting qualifications she had obtained in Ukraine were not properly recognized in England. This meant either being content with the lowest positions for the rest of her life or starting her studies from scratch and getting equivalent English qualifications. Of course, ambitious Lana chose the second path. She decided not to waste time on simple tests and chose the most recognised, but also the most difficult accounting qualification.

'There are fourteen exam papers,' Lana told her daughter while walking in the park. (Freeda raised her eyebrows and rolled her eyes). 'Two exam sessions each year,' Lana continued. 'So, I give myself five years to pass all the exams. What do you think?' She looked at Freeda with hope.

'Have you told Neil?' the little rascal asked.

'Not yet,' Lana replied. 'I'm going to do that tonight.'

***

'Five years? This is such a big commitment!' was Neil's first reaction.

'Hey!' Nicky reacted quickly. 'Approve immediately before she changes her mind, otherwise she will have nothing to do, and will only distract you from football!'

The very next moment, Neil agreed that it was a very good idea.

Then events began to occur, which Neil later called coincidences, but Lana knew for sure it could not have happened without the help of the Universe.

Firstly, she was unexpectedly granted exemptions from five exams, leaving only nine of fourteen papers required. Then four examination sessions a year were introduced, instead of two, which made it possible to pass all exams faster. And after a few months, Lana was employed at a company that encouraged obtaining this qualification and paid for the very expensive training!

***

Years of hard work followed, with Lana working and studying at the same time. But all her exams were passed on the first attempt and with very high marks, one of which turned out to be the best in her country and the twentieth in the world! This achievement earned a cash prize from her company, and an article was written about her in the corporate newsletter.

Finally, the long-awaited professional qualification was received, and Lana was ready for new challenges.

'Instead of the planned five years, we did it in just two!' Lily declared proudly, adjusting the glasses on her nose.

'It was a team effort,' Nicky corrected her. *'Neil and I helped as much as we could!'*

To Neil's credit, it must be admitted that he tried his best to watch football as much as possible during these two years, so as not to distract his wife from studying and exam preparation. Of course, he was sincerely happy about all her achievements, opening a bottle of champagne on the night when the exam results were published.

Chapter 33: Tower Bridge

After two years living in England and being involved in her husband's real estate business, Lana realised that she missed her work as an accountant, and she yearned for all those debits, credits, and charts of accounts. After discussing with Neil, she started looking for an accountancy job, where she could practice her skills and reinforce the professional training she was currently doing.

Lana was certain, that with her strong CV, it would be easy to find a job. At first, she only applied for the top accounting positions at large corporations and waited eagerly for an invitation to interview. But, strangely, none of these companies was interested in such a super-specialist...

Then Lana decided to expand her search and began looking for work with a focus on three areas:

1. Accountants with knowledge of the Russian language. Finding something in this category seemed to her the most probable.

2. Employment in the local area. There were mostly small positions with low salaries, but Lana was even ready for that.

3. And finally was the most ambitious and unlikely category; a job in a large international company in London.

Unfortunately, this strategy did not yield the desired result, and then Lana subscribed to all possible mailings of vacancies and sent multiple copies of her resumé every day.

A month later, the owner of a small accounting practice located within a five-minute walk from Lana's house, invited her for an interview. They had coffee and chatted for a long time in the local pub, after which he promised to call her to inform about his decision, 'soon'. There was no call.

At least some interest was shown in me, Lana reassured herself.

This was followed by an invitation to an interview with the Chelsea Football Club group. This did not quite fit with the family values, as Neil was a fan of The Arsenal, but Lana put on a suit, especially acquired for the occasion, and went to London. There she was cross-examined extensively in Russian, and the next day her candidacy was rejected as "overqualified".

But then, like so often, Lily came to the rescue. She grabbed a sheet of paper and a pen, threw them on the desk in front of Lana and commanded: 'Write down what you want!'

Thinking for a moment, Lana took the pen and wrote:
1. London

2. Large international company
3. Salary (such-and-such)
4. Start work August 23 (Lana really did not want to cancel a visit from her sister and nephew, scheduled for August, so she wanted to start work on August 23 – the day after they would return home.)

Then she folded a sheet of paper in four, opened the linen drawer, which doused her with the scent of lavender, put the magic note in the farthest corner and forgot about it.

Lana trudged to the next interview in London unenthusiastically. She was asked to take an accounting test and then was questioned for an hour. She answered intuitively, since she still had some difficulty understanding English, but the next day she was invited to a second interview.

Immediately after the interview, Lana went to the shopping centre and bought herself a new dress, choosing her favourite design: blue with bright flowers. Suddenly, her mobile phone rang. It was her recruitment agent! The interview had been successful, and the company had made her an offer: salary such-and-such, tuition fees, different types of insurance, twenty-five-day holiday, annual bonus, and more!

Lily put a last tick on her checklist and...

Lana accepted the offer.

***

On August 24, her first day at work, Lana stopped at London Bridge, took a photo of Tower Bridge, smiled.
Life is so good!

Chapter 34: Cat

They lived in a rented house for a second year, but Lana dreamt of acquiring their own home. Unfortunately, their financial situation did not allow this; property was too expensive in England. This was very upsetting for Lana. She ran through various scenarios in her head to make her dream come true, but none of them looked realistic.

***

Lana had a magical New Year's tradition. As the old year finished, she wrote a wish on a small piece of paper, then burned it, put the ashes into a glass of champagne and drank the contents of the glass. Lana was sure all her previous wishes made this way had come true; although, in all honesty, she could not remember any of them.

New Year Eve 2016 was no exception. Candles, champagne, small pieces of paper and pens — everything was prepared in advance. The house smelled of delicious food, a Christmas tree sparkled; laughter and clinking of glasses could be heard constantly.

***

'Look, Nicky, they are looking forward to the New Year and hope it will be happy,' Lily said with a sigh.

'I see, Lily,' Nicky replied, also sad. 'They don't know yet that Neil's mother, Sheila, will pass away next year...' Nicky continued.

'What will happen to her cat? He will probably have to go to a cat sanctuary and be rehomed.'

Lily's eyes sparkled mischievously, and she said, 'I think I have an idea...'

When the clock began counting down the last minute of the outgoing year, Lily flew quickly to Lana and, clutching her hand, brought forth a note: "CAT."

***

"CAT," Lana read with surprise, but she had no time to think on it, there were only a few seconds left until the New Year. She quickly burned the piece of paper and drank it with a glass of champagne.

***

Lily jumped for joy and clapped.

'Nicky, let's fill the rest of Sheila's life with pleasant events.'

'Great idea!' Nicky replied. 'I'll arrange it!'

***

That year, Neil spent a lot of time with his mother. He visited her often and she was invited to family events, they went to football matches, and even took a trip to Stockholm together.

In return, Sheila invited him and his family to her villa in Portugal, where they spent two great weeks enjoying the sea, the sun, delicious food and, of course, football on TV.

Tragic news arrived out of the blue in October. Sheila had unexpectedly died, leaving them a legacy of the house… and a cat named Oscar.

***

After recovering from the shock, Lana immediately adopted the cat, first of all correcting his name. *Oscar… Osya… Monsya*. 'Monsya is the new name of our cat!' she solemnly informed the family.

The cat was absolutely indifferent on which name to ignore. But, in order to somehow relate to the new name, Monsya turned into a little monster – he began to piss in the corners, jump on tables and constantly claw the furniture.

Lana decided to start his re-education. In return, the cat declared war on her. Sometimes she was even afraid to stay alone with the cat! The battle continued until Lana read on the Internet that it is important for cats to feel they are loved. Lana realised that Monsya would change only when her own attitude towards him changed. Naturally, she completely changed her approach to Monsya.

And what about the cat? The cat had no intention of changing and continued to periodically piss in the corners, tear furniture, and jump on tables. But now he was doing this "lovingly". And from now on he was allowed to finish eating from his family's plates.

Chapter 35: Vitamin B12

After Sheila's death, Neil's siblings suggested that he and his family move to their late parents' house, to look after Oscar and live there until the house was sold. By this time, Freeda had graduated from high school, so there was no reason for them to stay in Essex. The family agreed and moved to Kent.

It was a large house with a huge garden, which was quite difficult to maintain. Lana and Neil hoped they would sell the house quickly, after which they would buy their own home. They even started looking out for properties in their chosen area. However, dealing with probate and inheritance formalities turned out to be a long process, especially because it was still necessary to deal with Sheila's other possessions.

Lana decided. *As long as we live in this house, I will treat it as my own.*

She tried to maintain order, decorated, and regularly moved the furniture. The house seemed to sense it and began to reciprocate.

'Look out the window!' said Lana to her daughter, entering her room one morning. Looking out, Freeda saw an extraordinary picture: five little foxes were frolicking in the garden, their parents watching over them. The family came to the garden every day until the cubs grew up. After that, only the daddy fox continued to visit them regularly, and it was even given a nickname: Kevin.

At the back of the garden there was a small fishpond with an old bench next to it. Lana often went there with a cup of coffee to dream about her future home.

The house was convenient for Lana to prepare for her accountancy exams. When she got bored in one room, she moved to another, but only after she had moved everything in it that could be moved, put things in order, and opened the windows to let in some fresh air.

Monsya also supported Lana as best he could. For some reason, her textbooks and notebooks became his favourite resting place and, on waking up, Monsya demanded Lana open the window. She did it, gladly – watching his cute poses relaxed her and distracted her from the pressure of studying.

Occasionally, between exams and when her job permitted, Lana went with Neil on his football trips to European cities. One of the matches was played in Sweden, after which they were going to spend several days in Stockholm.

"Life is good!" Neil often repeated his favourite phrase.

Everything really looked very good. Lana hoped for a promotion after completing her qualifications, Freeda was successfully studying at one of the best universities in England, they planned to buy a house…

It seemed everything was moving in the right direction, and nothing could stop it.

***

But disturbing news came unexpectedly from Odessa. Lana's beloved sister, Tina, was urgently taken to the hospital after her health began to sharply deteriorate. The real problem was that the doctors could not give a diagnosis and, accordingly, did not know how to treat her. The tentative diagnosis, which they were not very confident in announcing, sounded very worrying.

'If all the money we get from the sale of the house must be spent on Tina's treatment, we will do it!' Neil said. 'And we will rent a house, millions of people live happily in rented property.'

This idea also flashed across Lana's mind, but only once. After that, she put it out of her head, and there was no more room for such a scenario.

Now, though, she thought, *I will have both - my own home and a healthy sister!*

"Think well, do well, and all will be well!"

Lana loved to repeat the principle that guided her all her life. She was sure that this time it would not let her down either.

***

'I like her train of thought!' Lily declared, proud of her ward.
'Yes, we are lucky with her,' Nicky agreed. 'She understands that everything starts with the mind.'

***

After being discharged from the hospital, Tina was sent to Kiev for a consultation with a professor who was considered one of the best specialists in her suspected illness in all of Ukraine.

However, he could not give definitive on the diagnosis and suggested Tina have further tests. After receiving the results of that test, she would need to book another appointment with him.

***

On Tina's birthday, Lana sat with a cup of coffee at London airport, waiting for a flight to Stockholm, where Neil was already waiting for her. As she sat there, emails began to arrive with the results of her sister's tests. After reading the diagnosis, Lana immediately started researching it on the Internet, and what she saw shocked her. It was a very bad diagnosis. Skimming quickly through a couple of articles, she told herself, *Stop! Stop reading this!* and disconnected her phone.

She was not used to feeling so constantly unhappy and worried. She decided to try to forget about the awful implications for a few days and spend the best time possible with Neil in Stockholm.

***

The capital of Sweden welcomed them with open arms. The weather was magical: everything was covered with snow, but at the same time it was quiet and warm.

Their hotel was near the Royal Palace, which they visited on the first day. Lana also found a wonderful guide. In just a couple of hours, the guide made them fall in love with both the city and the country, and she also advised the best restaurants for local cuisine.

Then there was the Vasa Museum and the ABBA Museum – after which Lana posted pictures on Facebook and one of her friends noted that Lana and Tina looked like Frida and Agnetha! Green-eyed and brown-haired Lana, and blue-eyed, blonde Tina really did resemble them. This comment made Lana's fears rise, but she immediately suppressed those thoughts.

Lana and Neil enjoyed the city, each other's company, and tried their best to avoid discussing such a painful topic.

***

I would like the professor to find that the diagnosis from laboratory tests is not clear!

Lana was thinking on the way to work on the day when Tina had her next appointment with the professor. Lana could think of no alternative. All the tests diagnosed the same illness, but Lana refused to believe them.

'The task is clear!'
Lily reacted instantly.
The pair flew to Tina's test results and shuffled the numbers in the graphs.

Lana received a message from her sister after she left the professor.

'Don't worry, everything is fine!'

Later, Tina called and told her that something in the findings of tests seemed contradictory, so the professor could not yet confirm the diagnosis. Lana was not surprised at all, because she herself came up with such a scenario and even managed to believe in it!

But the problem remained unsolved – there was no exact diagnosis, which meant there was still no treatment.

Lana began to insist that her sister come to England for an examination. Tina strongly resisted; she did not want to cause inconvenience to Lana and her family.

'Without the right diagnosis, they will cure you to death!' Lana continued to argue to persuade her sister.

Tina tried to defend the local doctors.

'No, I think it's just some kind of virus. Eventually, they will find the cause and prescribe the right treatment.'

Lana lost her patience.

'Well, then this "virus" has damaged your brain!'

For some reason, this phrase had a magical effect on Tina, and the very next day she agreed to come to England for examination.

***

Neil arranged everything: he found a private clinic that agreed to take on a foreign patient, forwarded translations of the examination results, in which Lily and Nicky had put all the numbers back in their correct places.

Lana met Tina at the airport; 'My lovely sister has arrived!'

Tina could barely carry her heavy travel suitcase, as its retractable handle had broken during transportation. Neil immediately took the bag from her, and Lana removed the belt from her beautiful blue floral dress and tied it to the handle of the suitcase to make it easier for her husband to carry it.

***

The sisters spent the next day in London.

Lying on the grass in Hyde Park, they discussed facial wrinkles and how to deal with them, avoiding talk about the main reason for Tina's visit in every possible way.

They went to the doctor all together: Tina, Lana, and Neil. Lana was supposed to act as an interpreter, but it turned out that there was no need for her assistance, since Tina translated her medical history into English and read it herself with expression. *What a clever girl!* Lana thought, looking at her sister with delight.

Smiling, the doctor listened carefully to Tina's story, after which he said that, judging by the account and the findings of the tests provided, he did not agree with the original diagnosis. Instead, he believed that the problem was simply a lack of vitamin B12, but he could only confirm this after an examination performed in their clinic. The necessary tests were done and, the very next day, the suspected diagnosis was confirmed, and treatment prescribed.

***

During the rest of the days of Tina's visit, they walked and laughed a lot, and even visited Freeda at the university so that Tina could see a student's life in England.

Lana told her sister funny stories about her wrong English pronunciation. 'Can you imagine? I kept telling him: "I have created new shit" instead of "I have created a new sheet."' They laughed long and loudly, to tears. Lana only laughed like that with her sister.

'How can you laugh like that?' Freeda asked. 'I can't do that. Teach me!'

Monsya also liked Tina. Every evening, he jumped on her lap and stayed there for a long time, purring loudly, and looking insolently at his family, who could only dream of such adoration from their own cat.

***

After Tina's departure, Lana switched back to dreaming about her own home, with her conscience clear.

Chapter 36: Coffee and Biscuit

They had completely different interests: Lana loved art, classical music, books, and guided tours – Neil was interested only in football. But he always kept her company when she invited him to her cultural events.

'Look, that bunny loves classical music. Can you see how attentively it listens?' he whispered quietly in his wife's ear during a classical music concert, pointing to a toy rabbit with raised ears in the arms of a little girl on the opposite side of the auditorium.

During the intermission, Neil feigned indignation. 'The drummer is a close relative of the conductor, for sure. He hit the drum only a couple of times during the whole concert, but probably gets the same salary as everyone else!'

He always made Lana laugh with his comments but, at the same time, he patiently endured many events that must have seemed boring for him, giving her the opportunity to enjoy them.

'Are you sure that he's an artist?' Neil jokingly asked Lana after visiting one of the art exhibitions. 'I can draw like that. Even a five-year-old can draw like that!'

'You don't have to like everything!' Freeda defended the artist. 'Visiting different exhibitions, we just learn more

161

about different directions of painting and only then decide what we like and what we don't.'

Lana was very pleased to hear this from Freeda – her efforts to instil a love of art in her daughter had not been in vain.

Every Christmas, 'Santa Neil' presented Lana with a wall calendar with reproductions of her favourite artists' paintings, and for her birthdays she received tickets to the best musicals. It was also customary that birthdays and family holidays were celebrated on days when there was no football - which sometimes required careful scheduling.

***

Freeda's seventeenth birthday coincided with the FA Cup final – Arsenal vs Aston Villa. Neil only managed to get one additional ticket, which he handed to the birthday girl as a gift.

'You can't even imagine how lucky you are!' he told her enthusiastically. 'Millions of people would like to be in your place on this day at Wembley!' Freeda did not share her dad's enthusiasm but went to the football.

Much to Neil's delight, Arsenal thumped Aston Villa 4-0 to win the trophy, which was presented to the team captain by Prince William.

'How lucky you are! You saw the prince!' Lana said to her daughter when they returned home.

'Which prince?' Freeda asked in surprise. It turned out that she spent almost the entire match on her phone and saw neither the match or the prince!

***

Unlike Freeda, Lana showed a greater respect for football while attending matches with Neil. Wearing a red and white Arsenal scarf, she was not on her phone, but simply daydreaming – which meant sometimes showing the wrong emotions and rejoicing in a goal scored by the opposing team, as she did not follow the game.

'You're like my mum,' Neil would say, laughing at such moments. 'She also always supported the other team.'

At one of the matches, Lana sat next to Derek, Neil's friend, and he told her about their family tradition: every weekend he brought tea to his wife, Angela, in bed and they discussed their plans for the day.

Lana loved this morning ritual and decided to immediately implement it in her family. 'But, instead of tea, please bring me coffee,' she told her husband.

'Are you really my friend?' Neil asked Derek jokingly. 'You are a very bad influence on my wife!'

But on the very first Saturday, he got up early and brought Lana coffee in bed.

'Where's the biscuit?' Bulochka asked, inspecting the delivery. Next time, the coffee was served with a biscuit.

Then a beautiful tray and a cup were bought especially for this ceremony from a tourist shop in an English castle.

'Wrong cup!' Bulochka was indignant if Neil accidentally brought coffee in another cup.

Bulochka's other frequently repeated remarks were: 'Lana does not eat spoons!' and 'This is not a biscuit; this is a cake!'

Once, in a film, Lana saw coffee served in bed with a flower in a small vase.

'Where is the flower?' Bulochka queried at the next morning coffee.

Neil approached the correction very creatively; now on the tray with coffee and biscuit there was a pot plant, a huge vase of flowers, or even just a bunch of basil!

All in all, Derek and Angela's nice custom became a kind of game for Lana and Neil, which filled their house with laughter and positive emotions every weekend.

Chapter 37: The Life-Changing Magic of Tidying Up

Finally, all the formalities of the inheritance were complete, and it was possible to start selling Sheila's house. Before each potential buyer arrived, Lana put the house in perfect order and opened the windows to let in a little autumn, winter, spring air. Many came to view, but no buyer emerged.

At the same time, Lana and Neil began to look for their own home, viewing several places each weekend. Lana subscribed to the mailing lists of all the estate agents in their chosen area, but she did not like anything for sale within their budget.

I don't want to live in a "shed"!

After receiving an email about the sale of another inexpensive house, Lana unsubscribed from all mailing lists.

'Everything is clear now! They need a more expensive house, which means they need to find money for it!' Lily formulated the task and began to fulfil it.

Lana had just passed her last exam and received the long-awaited qualification. She was immediately promoted from assistant accountant to accountant. In her new role, she improved existing accounting procedures and created new ones, implemented them with her team, and (thanks to a planning system in which she considered herself a master) all reporting was sent to the client within the agreed deadlines.

The client extolled the quality of work of Lana's team an expressed amazement during a telephone conversation with Lana. 'These are the best financial statements your company has ever drawn up for us! How did you manage to do all this in such a tight timeframe?'

You don't know me, yet! she thought. "Good planning is 90% of success," was a favourite phrase of Lana's – she invented it herself and followed it strictly. She really was a Master of Planning!

'She's not just a master of planning; she is a master of magical planning!' Lily bragged.
'She always writes down her plans, so we always know where our help is needed!'

Lana was very pleased with her achievements in her new role, but she was already dreaming about the next step – senior accountant. She did not just dream but felt and behaved as if she already was! Such a position became vacant unexpectedly, Lana immediately applied and was selected from several candidates.

'She got promoted twice just in a few months! Her salary has almost doubled!' Lily boasted.

'Now they'll get a bigger mortgage and be able to afford a better house.' Nicky agreed.

After receiving confirmation on the mortgage amount from the bank, they started to search for houses in a higher price bracket, and Lana liked them much more!
However, their dream house still eluded them.
If Lana liked one, Neil did not. The house Neil considered comfortable was not appreciated by Lana.
'By what criteria do you choose?' Neil asked, looking puzzled.
'I will FEEL our home,' his wife replied.
'I want us to buy Matisse's *The Dance* for our new home,' Freeda expressed.
'We'll buy the painting,' Lana replied, laughing. 'But first we have to find a house!'

'First you have to sell the house!' Nicky corrected her and, using his old trick, emailed Lana another link.

Having received an invitation to online training from the same friend who had recently helped her fall in love with her husband's football world, Lana accepted it without hesitation. From a relationship expert she was now retrained as an income coach, and that was exactly what Lana needed right now.

The homework for the first day of the course was to watch the film *The Life-Changing Magic of Tidying Up* and to sort out clothes after the show.

'Does it make my heart beat?' Lana asked herself aloud, taking out item after item from the pile of clothes on the bed, putting it to her heart, and laying it out in different directions depending on the answer.

'What are you doing?' Freeda asked, laughing at this scene.

'Don't disturb me!' Lana answered. 'It's a very important task, getting rid of things that no longer excite me.'

There were quite a lot of such clothes, even though Lana had never allowed herself to get cluttered. She regularly revised her wardrobe and donated clothes she had not worn for a long time to charitable organizations.

After finishing sorting out and hanging in the wardrobe the items that had passed the test, Lana opened the window, took a deep breath, and immediately felt that something new and wonderful was about to happen in her life.

***

'My heart starts to beat faster every time I see you,' Lana heard a voice from behind on the way to work the next morning.

Looking around, she saw a man of about seventy, dressed decently, whom she had never met before.

It turned out that he was a neighbour. He used to work in London, but then decided that it was not for him, and opened his own small accounting firm.

Having a pleasant conversation, they walked together to the square, where they parted ways – Lana to the station, and he to his office.

That evening, Lana told Neil about this unusual meeting. He was very surprised. Talking to a stranger on the street was completely uncommon for an elderly Englishman.

Lana never saw the man again.

Was he even there, she asked herself? The meeting was so strange.

***

Buyers for the house appeared the very next week: a married couple. It seemed odd because, until now, only large families with children had shown interested in the house.

'Let's go and see a place,' Neil said to Lana. 'I watched a house for a long time, but its price was much higher than our budget. Just yesterday it was significantly reduced.'

***

Lana did not FEEL the house. It was tired inside, with carpeted floors, which she could not abide. And it was obvious that the previous owners were smokers – the smell of tobacco had directly penetrated the walls and carpet.

But when Lana saw the garden, she was overwhelmed; She had never seen such beauty in her life!

The house stood at the edge of a wood, which began right behind the fence at the very end of the garden. Well-maintained plants, flowering rose bushes, a neatly-trimmed lawn, a terrace for garden furniture — everything looked so harmonious!

The garden consisted of two parts, which were separated by a low stone fence, and behind it (they could not believe their eyes!) there was a real, lively, gurgling stream with clear water!

'Well?' Neil asked hopefully, as they got back into the car.

Lana replied without hesitation.

'Yes! Yes! Yes!'

On the same evening, Bublik sent a video message to Freeda who was at her university: 'They found a house that they like and there is a wall in the house that you can hang Matisse on. We need to discuss it as soon as possible! Get in touch!'

Freeda was indignant on the phone, later that day.

'We have viewed so many houses together, and you didn't like any of them, but as soon as I left for university, you found a house at once! I have not even seen it!'

'Don't worry,' Lana reassured her. 'We will give you the largest bedroom in the house.'

Lana and Neil had decided to occupy a smaller room, the room overlooking the beautiful garden.

Chapter 38: A Home and a Business

Finally, Lana could relax. She had to wait only a couple of months until her dream to have her own house would come true —the time was needed to complete all the formalities associated with the sale of the old house and the purchase of the new one.

Some time ago, Neil had become interested in acquiring a new business, which had been offered to him on very favourable terms. More than once he had started a conversation with, 'Maybe it's better to acquire this business instead of a house? If it's successful, we will be able to afford a much better house.'

But Lana did not want to wait. She preferred a bird in a hand – not two in the bush. She wanted to have her own home, not someday, but now!

'Every time he starts such conversations, my heart just sinks. I really want my home!' she shared her worries with the same wise friend.

'What about having both a home and a business?' the friend asked.

'Oh no! It's impossible!' Lana replied. 'For the amount of money we have, it is unrealistic to get both.'

'Don't immediately say no; think first,' she heard in reply.

Lana decided to consider her friend's advice and not dismiss the idea of the possibility of buying both a house and a business – but sighed with relief when Neil made a choice in favour of a house.

Lana immediately began decorating and furnishing it in her mind's eye. A tape measure settled in her handbag next to her lipstick, waiting for the moment when it would be possible to start measuring everything in the new house.

In the evenings, they often drove up to their future home to admire it from outside.

'Is this really our home? I cannot wait!' Such moments made Lana emotional.

'Well, there is only a little time to wait,' Neil reassured her, laughing.

***

Lana was worried about the move, as they first had to get rid of all unnecessary items in the old house, and from the garage and sheds. She was horrified at the amount of work they had to do.

How can we cope with all this?!

***

'I wonder how Babushka is?' Lily asked softly. 'Probably bored, with nothing to do...'

'Nothing like that,' Nicky replied, realizing what she was driving at. 'Summer is in full swing in Odessa.

Babushka goes to the beach every day, swims, and sunbathes.'

'If she just needs the hot weather, I can organise that easily here, too!'

Lily had decided.

***

Summer in England that year was really very hot.

Babushka offered her help with the move. Lana booked her a flight the same day.

Together, they coped with the difficult task of clearing the house and outbuildings, although most of the work fell on the shoulders of the willing guest.

Lana and Neil were immensely grateful, and on Babushka's birthday, Neil booked a nice dinner at a fancy restaurant for the whole family.

***

On the day of the move, it was hard for Lana to concentrate on her work.

'Babushka asked us to buy some bread,' Neil said, meeting his wife at the station that day.

'No!' Lana replied immediately. 'I will not go; I want to go home!' He took her home, and then drove to get the bread.

Lana walked slowly through the new house, moving from room to room and examining everything carefully. She liked everything!

What lovely people! Lana thought.

The previous owners had left the house in perfect order: carpets, curtains, everything was clean. Even the smell of tobacco had disappeared. The lawn was trimmed neatly, and the stream cleared of debris.

Don't worry, we will also take good care of you and love you, she thought, mentally addressing the house.

***

Neil had read online tips for moving cats to a new home. 'To prevent Oscar from running away, we must not let him go outside at first.'

It made sense, but was difficult to do, since the heat made it impossible to keep the windows and doors closed all the time.

'I think we should allow him to go out into the garden, but under our supervision,' Babushka suggested. 'Oscar is a smart cat. He won't run away!'

One afternoon, while Neil was busy and not watching, Babushka decided to let Monsya out into the garden. She just felt so sorry for the cat living under lock and key. Examining the territory, accompanied by Babushka, Monsya moved into the depths of the garden, leapt over the fence and disappeared into the wood! Babushka called Neil for help.

Running into the wood, they saw Monsya peacefully browsing the grass. At that moment, two huge dogs appeared out of nowhere, and Monsya, frightened, ran up a tree.

'Where is he?' Babushka asked, trying to make out the cat in the dense foliage. Neil took a photo of two shining eyes and showed it to Babushka.

For the next several hours, they took turns watching the cat sleeping sweetly on a large branch of a tree. People passing by looked in amazement at the strange elderly woman sitting on a tree stump.

'Cat, Cat! Meow!' she tried to explain to them, using her limited knowledge of English and pointing to the tree.

'Is it a kitten?' one woman asked, bringing her hands close to each other, specifying in this manner the size of the runaway.

'No, no, not kitten! A cat!' Babushka replied, spreading wide her arms. Monsya really was a rather impressive size.

Some passers-by offered help, but Neil declined politely, hoping that Monsya would climb down on his own after his nap.

It began to get dark, but Monsya still did not climb down. Neil dragged a ladder over and, climbing it, delicately tried to reach the cat. But the cat would not even budge. After that, Babushka got down to business. She grabbed a long-handled broom, climbed the ladder and, despite Neil's protests, shook the branch. Monsya climbed down the trunk of the tree and jumped onto Neil's shoulder.

'If Neil had allowed me, I would have done it much earlier,' said Babushka when she told the story of the happy rescue to Lana and Freeda at dinner. Everyone laughed!

Monsya made one more attempt to escape into the wood, after which he realised finally that the area bounded by the fence was much safer.

The change of residence was not easy for the cat. His thick fur knotted into huge mats from stress, and Babushka cut them out every day until the fur finally became even.

In addition, he began to have problems with his teeth, and the poor cat could not eat because of the pain. Babushka cooked chicken broths especially for him, then he was taken to the vet.

'Oscar!' The patient was summoned to the veterinarian.

'Is he eating?' the veterinarian asked first. Then she saw the huge lump crawling out of the cage. 'Oh, I see he eats enough!'

Monsya needed several teeth removed, but recovered fully, much to the family's relief.

***

'I don't know how to wean him from this terrible habit of tearing up furniture,' Lana complained to Emily when she came to dinner one day.

'I know how to do it!' Emily said that if Lana lightly sprayed the cat with water from a spray bottle as soon as he was going to sharpen his claws on the furniture, he will gradually learn not to do it.

The very same evening Lana tested her newly purchased flower sprayer and named it "Emily" afterwards. Later, it turned out that "Emily" was also doing very well with the neighbour's cat, Timmy, who was stubbornly fighting Monsya for territory.

***

Supervising the renovation work was another responsibility of Babushka's, which she undertook voluntarily. Although the builders could not speak Russian and Babushka did not understand English, she somehow managed to give them clear advice and instructions.

'Tomorrow, they start installing the electrics, so tonight you have to mark where you will need the sockets," she said to Lana one day. Lana had already thought everything out in advance and quickly marked the walls with the correct positions. But when the sockets were completed, she realised that she had placed them in very inaccessible places in her bedroom – behind the bedside tables. While it was good that they were not clearly visible, the bedside tables had to be moved to access them, which irritated Lana.

'Move the dresser with the bedding to another room, and everything will become comfortable at once!' Nicky prompted.

Lana followed his advice during one of her periodic furniture rearrangements, moving the bed and bedside tables closer to the window, and (oh, miracle!) everything became very convenient.

In my house, even the sockets move by themselves!

***

After completing everything required of her, Babushka went home. Before she left, Oscar threw suddenly himself under her feet and she fell, hitting her eye hard.

'Is this your gratitude for everything I have done for you?' Babushka asked, putting ice to her eye.

'What's the matter?' Tina asked fearfully, meeting Babushka at Odessa Airport and pointing to her black eye.

'It is a gift from Oscar!' she answered with a laugh.

Lily defended the cat. 'He just didn't want you to leave!'

***

As for a new business, they did acquire it in a beautiful place, in the south of the country in Sussex. Lana loved to walk there along the coast of the English Channel, daydreaming, greedily breathing the salty sea air and listening to the calls of seagulls.

How I miss all this! she would think at these moments, remembering her beloved Black Sea in Odessa.

I want an apartment with a sea view!

Lana imagined herself sitting at a writing desk near a large window overlooking the endless surface of the water.

Chapter 39: William Blake

"The greatest English poet and the most original artist of the Romantic era, William Blake (1757-1827) always dreamed of painting large-scale canvas in churches and palaces, but, unfortunately, he never got this opportunity. More than two centuries after his death, Tate Britain announces that it is going to make the artist's dream come true – projecting Blake's last work, *The Ancient of Days,* onto the giant dome of St. Paul's Cathedral. Only available for three days, from November 29 to December 1! Do not miss this!" warned the hoarding.

When Lana read this, her heart began to quicken. She wanted so much to see this beauty with her own eyes! St. Paul's Cathedral was just fifteen minutes' walk from her office, but off her normal route.

If the dates fell on working days, then I could go there after work, she thought, opening the calendar. But, much to Lana's dismay, all the days were inconvenient: Friday night (when they had already agreed to meet Neil's friend), Saturday, and Sunday.

She tried to console herself. *Never mind, I'll go to Tate Britain for the exhibition.*

181

***

Lana's workplace was in the centre of the capital, right on the banks of the Thames near London Bridge, so she always tried to go out at lunchtime for a walk along the river and enjoy the impressive views of the City of London.

Friday, November 29 was no exception. The weather was nice, it was warm and sunny. Lana had a cup of coffee at a nearby cafe and headed back. That afternoon, she planned to check and send one more report to a client and go out for dinner with Neil and his friend in the evening.

Lana returned to the office around 2 o'clock. She was walking to her desk when she clearly heard gunshots – *!!* – followed a moment later by the sounds of sirens. She and her colleagues ran to the window overlooking London Bridge and saw a large white truck parked at a strange angle, blocking the road.

'Everyone, move away from the windows! All of you, move away from the windows immediately!' a loud voice commanded. The crowd gathered at the windows quickly dispersed to their desks, worriedly.

Lana messaged Neil.

We've got shots here and a lot of police cars. Can you google what happened?

His response came quickly.

It looks like a terrorist attack...

Within a few minutes, an order was given for everyone to move back from the windows as far as possible and into the middle of the office.

Lana quickly emailed her client, informing them that they would most likely not be able to send the promised report on time, and then joined everyone else at the back of the office.

Long hours of waiting began.

There were periodic calls from the police, which only reiterated that no one should approach the windows or leave the building.

News was gathered from the Internet and worried relatives. There were several terrorists and not all had been caught. They had suicide belts, and the white truck outside might be filled with explosives.

It soon became hot and stuffy in the office, due to the large crowd of people gathered in a small area, but everyone just sat and waited patiently; no one panicked. Unfortunately, terrorist attacks had become a part of life in London. Indeed, there was another incident just two years before, and in virtually the same place.

A fire alarm test took place in the office at 10 a.m. every Tuesday, and evacuation drills were carried out every few months. Everyone, like robots, would get up from their seats, abandoning

183

unfinished important tasks and, taking only the essential items, calmly leave the office and head to the agreed assembly place.

Once, the siren was not a training exercise, but real. A suspicious car had been discovered near the nearest underground station. In a matter of minutes, all nearby buildings were evacuated, and a huge stream of people, directed by the police, left the dangerous area.

Like a May Day demonstration, only the flags are missing, Lana thought at the time. Surprisingly, she had no fear then or now – or so she thought.

'We need to support her somehow,' Lily decided. 'I'll arrange a little surprise for her!'

While corresponding with Neil, chatting with colleagues, and dreaming, four hours of waiting passed (almost) smoothly. Finally, they were allowed to leave the building in small groups of five or six, through the back entrance, towards St. Paul's Cathedral.

The streets of London were unusually empty. Their group moved slowly along the Thames in the winter darkness, peering cautiously at the rare passers-by.

'Look! How beautiful!' one of her colleagues exclaimed, pointing to the dome of St. Paul's Cathedral, displaying the famous painting by William Blake, shining bright colours into the night.

    Lana just stared at the sight; it was so wonderful! She was fixated, but everyone else moved on and she had to follow them.

    On the way, the group gradually dissipated, everyone going on their own commute, and Lana was left alone with her colleague, Agnieszka.

    Closer to Westminster Bridge, life was in full swing, as if nothing had happened in London that day; music played, it was crowded, and the air was filled with the aroma of street food and mulled wine.

    'Let's stop for mulled wine!' Lana suggested.

    'And eat something,' Agnieszka agreed. It had been a long time since lunch.

    Having bought food and drinks, they settled on a bench overlooking the Thames and admiring the lights of London at night. Agnieszka talked about how she met her boyfriend and about their plans for the future; Lana shared the story of her romance with Neil and told her about their "Coffee and Biscuit" tradition, which Agnieszka immediately decided to adopt.

    Then they walked together to Waterloo station and went home.

***

At home, Neil immediately poured her a glass of red wine. Finally sitting comfortably, Lana suddenly felt extremely tired. As if sensing it, Monsya jumped onto her lap and curled up, turning on the purr at full volume.

Lana slowly drank the wine, stroked the cat, and tried to recall the events of that day. Nothing associated with the terrorist attack came to her mind, but she clearly remembered drinking coffee in a cafe, mulled wine, a happy conversation with Agnieszka on a bench near the Thames and, of course, the unforgettable sight of the famous Blake picture on the dome of St. Paul's Cathedral.

Lana thought, sadly, *I dreamt of seeing it and saw it… But at what cost!*

Two people were killed and three more injured in the terrorist attack that took place in London on November 29, 2019.

Chapter 40: Bristol, or the New Wizard

Freeda's university years passed quickly. She made some good friends, and she enjoyed all the freedom and joys of student life while finding the right balance between entertainment and study.

Although her academic achievements were more than impressive, she did not always manage her time well, leaving everything to the last moment.

'How do you manage everything?' she once asked her mother. 'Teach me.'

And Lana, this "master of magic planning," set immediately to work and began with her favourite phrase. 'Good planning is 90% success!'

'First, assess how much work you need to do and how much time you have for it. Then count how many questions you need to learn per day, so you have time for revision and rest. The day before the exam, do nothing, let your brain relax. Most importantly, try to stick to your plan. In the evenings, make the list for the following day. Write everything down! Then it will be easier for the Universe to help you.'

Gradually, Lana began to see the results of her lessons of good planning – calendars with to-do lists, lecture schedules, and paragraphs hung beautifully on the walls of her daughter's room.

Freeda also came in handy with her mother's knowledge of finance.

Lana and Neil were waiting in the pub for their daughter to return from the financial accounting exam, for which Lana had helped her prepare. Lana said, 'I want to hear her say, "I knew everything!"'.

An hour later, a happy student came rushing in and declared, with joy, 'For the first time in my life, I knew everything and answered all the questions!'

***

As Freeda grew older, mother and daughter shared many common interests: they travelled together, attended exhibitions and concerts, enjoyed similar taste in food, and argued less often.

What a good friend I have raised for myself! Lana thought, with pride.

But there was more to be proud of. Her daughter had become a beautiful, intelligent, independent girl with her own opinions and a great sense of humour. In addition to her appearance, Freeda inherited empathy and the ability to make friends from her biological father. In her world, as in the world of her father, there were many true, sincere, and devoted friends.

***

Freeda graduated from university with first class honours. After that, she faced a choice. What next? Continue studying or look for a job? Where would she work? London, or somewhere else?

Lana had believed that it would be very difficult to find a job in the face of endless coronavirus lockdowns, so it would be right to do a master's degree in London and live at the family home. But she was no longer as certain as before.

'We will support any decision you make,' she told her daughter.

The problem was that Freeda herself did not know what she wanted. The only thing she knew for sure: she did not want to live with her parents. Having experienced independent life at university, she craved more.

'I will look for a job!' she decided.

***

Lana and Freeda were walking locally on a quiet September evening. Mum's working day was just over, and her daughter was still looking for work, which turned out to be very difficult during COVID quarantine.

'I am so bored of looking for work!' Freeda complained. 'I've submitted a hundred CVs, but still no job!'

'Have you already decided on the city and what kind of job you want?' Lana asked.

'Oh, if I knew! Bristol, London? I just can't decide,' Freeda replied.

'How can the Universe help you if you don't know yourself? Come home and clearly write down what you want.' Lana recommended her magic method, proven more than once.

Surprisingly, Freeda did not argue. She was already accustomed to the fact that the dreams and plans of her mother (and grandmother, too!) came true in some magical way. Although Neil thought these wins were just coincidence, Freeda had long begun to suspect everything was not quite as simple as that.

'How do you do it? Why is it so easy for you?' she asked.

'Because I am a wizard!' she answered, laughing.

Freeda did not object to that either.

'You are a wizard. Babushka is a wizard. What about me?' she asked, looking hopefully at her mother.

Lana answered without hesitation.

'And you are a wizard! The main thing is to believe, notice miracles, and enjoy them. Then there will be more and more of them in your life.'

Freeda thought she would not mind being a good witch.

Arriving home, the newly-made enchantress took out a sheet of paper and began to write:

1. Job in Bristol

Then she added items two and three. The final list turned out to be quite long.

She also did not forget to wish for her friend, India.

If it's magic, so let it be magic! Freeda thought, adding more and more items to her list of miracles.

***

'Another one is ready! Next!' commanded the chief angel, and a couple of little angels flew up to Freeda.

'What a pretty one!' said the angel girl.

'It doesn't matter what she looks like,' the angel boy grumbled. 'All that matters is she believes in miracles.'

Thus, Freeda received her own guardian angels, her own Lily and Nicky, who became responsible for all the miracles in her life.

***

The very next day she was invited for an interview with a company from Bristol.

'My chances are practically zero there,' Freeda complained to her parents after reading the information about this job. 'Almost four hundred candidates have already applied!'

'Don't think about it! Prepare well for the interview and try to get through it as well as possible,' Lana advised, handing her daughter one of her office blouses.

***

A few days after the interview, Lana and Freeda flew to Sicily. Although the weather forecast threatened rain, they decided not to cancel the trip. First, it was one of the few places where there were no coronavirus restrictions, and second, having grown up by the Black Sea, they needed a seaside holiday at least once a year.

The very first day in Sicily was marked by long-awaited, excellent news: Freeda successfully passed the interview and was offered the job in Bristol!

For the rest of the holiday, they just enjoyed the warm sea, gentle sun, and delicious Sicilian food. They were even very lucky with the weather – it rained, but at night.

***

The next item on Freeda's magic list was her friend, India. They wanted to move to Bristol together and, for that, India also needed to find a job. Surprisingly, she succeeded after just one interview.

Together, they quickly found an apartment in a beautiful house on the banks of the Avon River, which they were supposed to move into with three young people of similar age.

***

Having loaded their daughter's personal effects into the car, the parents drove her to her new home.

Freeda received a message on her way to Bristol. Her friend, James, was the first to check in and immediately shared his impressions with the rest. 'It's too good to be true!'

The apartment really was very good: a spacious living room with large windows overlooking a green, a modern kitchen, cosy bedrooms, beautiful bathrooms.

It turned out that James had started looking for housing in Bristol a long time ago and had viewed a huge number of apartments, but none of them compared with this one that Freeda and India found.

'How did you find it?' he asked them. Lana and her daughter exchanged a glance. They knew how it worked in the world of enchantresses!

After enjoying a glass of champagne with Freeda and her new friends, the parents went home, leaving their daughter to her new adult life.

Chapter 41: Lily and Nicky

Lana had everything she needed to be happy: a loving and beloved husband, a clever daughter, a comfortable house with a beautiful garden, an interesting and well-paid job, the world's most prestigious accounting qualification, and even a cat.

She asked herself, *What's next?*

Everything she dreamt of had come true. Yes, all her life Lana worked hard, set goals, and walked confidently towards them. But she also always felt the tremendous support and love of the Universe, which generously showered her with its miracles.

Lana wrote on a piece of paper, asking either herself or the Universe, *What is my mission in life?*

Lily answered in invisible ink.
"Encourage other people to see miracles in their lives!"

Miracles, of course, miracles!
Lana was delighted. *I have to find a way to teach people to believe in miracles and notice them!*

She looked back at her life and realised that help always came when it was needed. The Universe did its job, and then rested, watching the happiness of a woman who sincerely believed in magic. Even during dark periods, Lana felt the great love and care of the Universe. This manifested itself in small daily miracles that delighted her, although her husband called it all just coincidences.

What can I do to help people notice miracles in their lives? Lana continued her dialogue with the Universe.

Lily brought out her magic ink and beautiful, neat handwriting.
"Write a book!"

***

The next morning, Lana woke up with a clear decision to start writing a book.

'The book will be about miracles in my life!' she told her family, choking with delight. 'I will describe the help of the Universe through two angels — a girl and a boy. The girl will be based on Bulochka, and the boy will be Bublik. I just need to come up with names for them.'

***

That same day, the whole family went for a walk to the coast. The daughter rattled nonstop, Neil kept up the conversation politely, and Lana wrote the first chapters of her book in her mind.

Someone called loudly, interrupting the harmonious stream of Lana's thoughts.

'Lily! Come!'

'Lily! The angel girl will be called Lily!' Lana happily informed Neil and Freeda. 'What should I call the boy then? Lily and...'

'Nicky,' Neil suggested.

'Lily and Nicky! Exactly what I need!' The new writer was delighted.

In the car on the way home, Lana opened the notes on her phone and began to work, inspired by this new chapter of her amazing life:

Chapter 1: God Exists!

When Lana was five years old, her mother taught her to dream...

Acknowledgements

First of all, I want to thank my Mum, whose boundless love, faith, and support throughout my life has given me tremendous strength, energy, motivation, and courage to move forward and try new things. You were there at all stages of this book and your help is always invaluable.

Also, many thanks to my dear and beloved husband, Neale. I am immensely happy and grateful to fate that I met you on my path in life. You have given me the most beautiful and magical chapters of my life and my book. I love you and I feel your love.

Special thanks to my daughter, Alina — my little rascal, called Freeda in this book. Through her often caustic, but truthful remarks, the Universe sends its messages. My daughter is not a copy of me, but a self-sufficient person looking for her own path, with her own opinions, and a huge inner strength. I love you immensely, I believe in you, and I am proud of you.

Thanks to my beloved sister, Tatyana. You are my angel! I will never cease admiring your kindness, tact, and sincerity. Your continued support in the process of writing this book gave me the belief that someone needs it, and the book will find its readers.

Thanks to the first readers of the book and my wonderful friends; Lyudmila Stetsenko, Victoria Niklaus, Oksana Bachynska, Oksana Titova and Anna Mikhaylyuchenko. With your supportive comments, you gave me confidence that I was on the right track.

Svetlana Malezhik - The book is filled with your presence, although I do not mention your name in it. Thank you, my dear friend and mentor!

Elena Lyubynska - It was you who transformed my dream of writing a book into action by writing "Write a book!" on my kitchen board one magical Christmas night. In the last chapter of the book, Lily does it for you. Thank you!

I have met a huge number of wonderful people, each of whom contributed something important and valuable to my life. I am sure many of you will recognize yourself in this book. I thank you from the bottom of my heart; I remember and appreciate your contributions to my treasury of miracles!

Lana O'Nealova
2023

Printed in Great Britain
by Amazon